SOME ARE SHADOWS

A novel by

DAVID SAYRE

ISBN: 0692659358
ISBN 13: 9780692659359
Library of Congress Control Number: 2016935169
U. S. ISBN Agency, New Providence, NJ

ACKNOWLEDGEMENTS

To the loving family and friends who are always there for me, an endlessly grateful thank you. Big things, small things, all things... none are possible without the people in our lives.

Prologue

Last Breath

"Oh Lord have mercy, this is a dirty floor."

How strange, she thought to herself, for that to be the phrase running through her mind at these, the final moments. Not wondering what would be waiting for her after it ends, not thinking about the worry and the grief those who loved her would feel. But that the floor was dirty. And she knew it would be, but it was honestly something she had not been preoccupied with until this moment. No, the cleaning woman she had paid twelve dollars a week was not due until the following morning. Come to think of it, her housemaid was most likely the person that would find her lying here in whatever condition she would ultimately be left.

Her last gasps of breath, a pair of gloved, strong hands forcefully gripped around the circumference of her neck, and the only thought she could entertain as she drifted into darkness was... "I am going to die on this dirty floor."

CHAPTER 1

THE GUMSHOE

"**H**ow come no sauerkraut today?"

The vendor shrugged as he opened his metal tongs and dipped into the steaming vat, pulling out a hot dog to place on a bun for his next customer. "A dog should have sauerkraut," Sheen reiterated.

Benjamin Sheen liked a big scoop of sauerkraut and a lot of mustard on his hot dog. Often he would go the extra mile and pile some chopped onions on, when they were available. He firmly believed that a hot dog was only worth eating when you needed at least three napkins to clean up the mess.

"Cabbage shortage," replied the aging, sun-tanned hot dog vendor. "You know how it is. The commies, they're taking over everything!" Sheen smirked at the hard working frankfurter peddler.

"You think you're being wise, pal. But I know you're lying to me."

The vendor pointed his closed tongs at Sheen and asked, "How many times you bought lunch off of me?" Sheen shrugged and replied, "Three times a week for the past two years."

The vendor nodded, "And how many times I been outta sauerkraut?"

"Never."

"Okay, then! You wanna stop busting my chops?"

"Just trying to keep you honest," quipped Sheen. The vendor rolled his eyes and opened an ice filled compartment on the opposite end of his hot dog cart. "You want your bottle of Nehi, or not?"

Sheen chuckled. "Orange." The vendor pulled out an ice-cold bottle and popped the top off with the bottle opener he kept chained to the cabinet on the back of the cart.

"See you next time," Sheen said as he walked away, leaving the vendor to raise his hand in the simple gesture of farewell before tending to the next hungry consumer.

The hot dog stand that Sheen preferred was on the corner of Biscayne Boulevard and Northeast 6th street, right in front of the Miami News Building. The humor of this was not lost on Sheen as he gave five cents to the kid selling copies of the Miami Herald two blocks away. But The Miami News was an evening paper, the new edition would not be out for several hours and it was Sheen's ritual after lunch to read through the pages as he walked the five blocks south to his office.

He skimmed through the front page information. The major headline for June 2, 1952 was the steel workers strike that was expected to begin. Estimations of half a million or more workers would stand on the picket line for wage increases. In local news, the filing deadline for the upcoming gubernatorial election had been the night before and a republican from Gainesville by the name of Delmar Wiggins had thrown his hat in the ring to challenge the sitting governor, a democrat and former mayor from Miami, Nathaniel Eldridge.

Some might have thought that walking the five blocks north and two blocks east was a bit long for a lunchtime hot dog, but Sheen liked it. Mostly because it gave him a round trip that took time... time to be out of the office and clear his head. A nearly meditative method that helped Benjamin most when he was working on a difficult case.

As he turned the corner off of 1st avenue, heading towards North Miami Avenue, he thumbed through the black and white print to find the sports pages. Everyone who followed the game of baseball was wondering if the Yankees could win their fourth straight world series this year, despite being the first season they would play in fifteen years without Joe DiMaggio. Joltin' Joe had announced his retirement during the winter. But last year's rookie, Mickey Mantle, looked promising and the Bombers still had Yogi Berra, Gil McDougald and Phil Rizzuto. Of course, in this town, all the baseball talk was focused on the great start the Miami Sun Sox, a minor league team for the Brooklyn Dodgers, had gotten off to. They were leading the pack in the Florida International League with their closest competition being that of their cross-town rivals, the Miami Beach Flamingos.

Sheen had reached the front door of the building at 36 Northeast 1st Street and by the time he reached his door on the fifth floor marked Benjamin Sheen, Private Investigator, he would have read all the news he deemed necessary. His gentle, green eyes, the clearest indicator of his Irish ancestry, batted back and forth as he processed the words on the page. With rhythmic precision, he would glance up as he made the turn at each banister that marked the progress of the incline along the stairs. His long face wore a ruddy complexion, the next feature indicative of his genealogy. The expression was usually one of curiosity, if not contemplation.

He opened the door to his offices and removed his grey, pinch-front, teardrop-shaped crown fedora, revealing his closely cropped, neatly combed light-brown hair. He placed his hat on the hat rack, noticing that a black pork-pie style cap was hanging from one of the arms. Before he had the chance to ask Mrs. Skeffington about it, his loyal secretary volunteered an explanation. "There is a colored man in your office," she said with a slight gulp that nearly became a gasp, though she tried to hide her concern.

"Oh, really," Sheen asked. "What color?" The sweet, conventional woman, who wasn't nearly old enough to be Sheen's mother, though she might as well have been with the way she doted on him, gave a flustered sigh at his rhetorical question.

"Never mind," Sheen offered as he walked past her desk to his personal office. "I'll find out myself."

Sheen entered his office to find a stocky black man in his early thirties, about ten or eleven years Sheen's junior, sitting in the wooden chair that rested in front of the detective's desk. The man was well-dressed for a Negro, Sheen thought. Nothing fancy, but certainly not lower working class. He wondered who this fellow was and what business had brought him here.

"Wendell Childress," he uttered as he extended his hand. Sheen was quick to accept and shake. He had long ago made it a habit not to stare at the outstretched hand of a black man, wondering whether or not he wanted to touch it. His father had always reacted that way and so had his grandfather and plenty of other men he had known in his life. Sheen was never sure why that bothered him so much, but it did. Not that Benjamin didn't have his share of discomfort towards blacks, after all he had been raised as a man in the south by two generations of men who were definitively "deep south". But his conflicted feelings about coloreds were far more subconscious, a product of the culture of his upbringing, and something he didn't, or tried not to pay much attention to.

"Benjamin Sheen. What can I do for you, Mr. Childress?" he asked as he sat down behind his desk. Childress reclaimed his seat across from the private detective.

"My sister was murdered, and I am still lookin' for answers to her death," Childress said with a furrowed brow.

"The police are investigating, aren't they?"

4

"They was for a while. But seems they can't find nothin' else past what they started out with."

"When was she killed?"

"Her body was found on February the nineteenth."

"Over three months ago. Who was it that found your sister?"

"A domestic. She come in to clean one morning and found Henrietta lyin' on the floor."

"Henrietta, that's your sister's name?" Sheen confirmed as he wrote the name on a pad of paper that was always at the ready amidst the contents scattered upon his desk. "Yes, sir," Wendell replied.

He reached into his coat pocket and pulled out a photograph, handing it to the detective. Sheen examined the picture of a startling beauty with enchanting almond eyes and strong, high cheekbones that accentuated a slim face upon a long, shapely neck. Her hair was just above shoulder length. It had been straightened, probably with lye. And her smile was a peculiar yet inviting one. As if she knew you were looking at her in amazement of her looks and charm, but the personal satisfaction of that fact was her own little secret to keep. Sheen reacted to the picture, "Pretty girl." He studied it a moment longer before stating, "Funny... she looks awfully familiar."

Wendell nodded and smiled, "You maybe recognize her from the flicker shows. Her stage name was Etta Childs."

"Is that right?" Sheen asked. "What pictures?"

"*The Homesteaders. First Train Out.*" Wendell could tell by Sheen's blank expression as he tried to make the connection that the detective had never heard of these movies. Truth be told, Wendell didn't expect him to know them. These were the independent black movies that Etta had starred in and they typically were not released in mostly white theaters. But Wendell had to mention them first because they were the ones Etta loved the most. And, by God, they were Wendell's favorites too, because these were the movies where his older sister played the lead role in pictures with honest portrayals of black folks. Of course, most white audiences would probably only recognize her from movies where she played a supporting part, and usually as a singer on-stage in some night club scene.

"*Matinees and Melodies*," Wendell asked with a raised eyebrow, assuming Sheen would know this one. Sheen snapped his fingers and smiled, "Yeah! That Ray Denton picture, where he played the speakeasy owner. Sure, sure... she sang, uh... Stormy Weather, right?"

Wendell nodded, "That was my sister."

"I'll be a son of a gun." Sheen held up the photo, "You mind if I hang onto this picture?"

"As long as I get it back, Detective."

"Of course," Sheen replied as he placed the photo next to his notepad. "Got any idea what the homicide squad is doing with the investigation?"

"Well see, that's why I come to you. I went down to the station Tuesday last and they tell me it's an open file, but lest they come upon new evidence they can't do nothin' more. I 'spect somebody else got they selves killed and the police got more important people to investigate for, but I am trying hard as I can to think kindly on the situation."

"Who is working the case for Homicide?"

"Detective Tierney. He seems to be a decent man."

"Mm-hmm." Sheen agreed that Tierney was a decent man. In fact in all the time they worked together in the vice squad, when Sheen carried a badge for the city of Miami police department, he always felt that Tierney was a stand-up detective that would eventually be promoted to the department's highest calling in criminal investigation. Clearly, he was not wrong.

"You say the murder took place at your sister's house?"

"Yes, sir."

"I thought all those movie stars lived out in Hollywood."

"I can't rightly say nothin' for them other folks, but Henrietta said she always wanted to keep a place here at home."

"I understand. One last thing... can you think of anyone who might want to see your sister killed?"

"No, sir."

"I know it's difficult to think about and, believe me, I don't want to make things embarrassing... but the more I know, the better prepared I am for an investigation. A jilted lover, perhaps? Somebody around town... did she owe any money?"

"Mr. Sheen, as far as I know Henrietta didn't have enemies. She just wasn't that type. Girl would give you the shirt off her back if'n she thought it could help you. I can't think of a single person who would have a mind to cause her harm."

It always started like this, Sheen thought. Some poor soul comes in looking to right a wrong, usually a dead loved one, or at least someone who is missing... But they don't know about the person's life outside of their relationship. Or maybe they don't want to know, and if they do, it's too painful to accept the reality after their loss.

"All right," Sheen said. "Here's what we'll do... I can go ahead and look around, see if I come across anything. Now I get twenty dollars to start an inquiry. After that, it's forty bucks a week. Is that a problem for you?"

"No, Mr. Sheen. Money is no question. I just want to know what happened to Henrietta," Wendell unequivocally stated.

"Okay. In the meantime, I want you to take the next few days and think about all the people you know of that are friends, acquaintances... anybody, particularly around town, that knew your sister. Once you've put that list together, you let me know. Got a number where I can contact you?"

Wendell nodded. Sheen tossed the notepad and a pencil across the desk. He didn't have to give any further instruction, Wendell understood. He picked up the pencil and jotted down a couple of phone numbers. He handed the pad over to the detective and explained, "That first number is the number at the house. The second one is the number for my diner."

"Oh? What diner is that?" Sheen asked.

"The 7th Street Diner. It's in Overtown."

"You own this place?"

"Yes sir. Like I said, Henrietta was a generous soul."

"And she gave you the money to open?"

"Yes."

"How's business going?"

"Real swell."

"Good for you." Sheen stood up and walked around the desk towards Wendell. The detective's new client took the hint and stood up as well. Sheen extended his hand, "I'll be in touch, Mr. Childress." They shook hands as Wendell replied, "Thank you, Detective."

Sheen ushered Wendell out of the office and returned to his own quiet thoughts. He asked himself what he knew about Etta Childs... not much. She had been a movie star, apparently bigger in some circles than in others. She was black, she was local and she was dead. Not much at all. So it was down to asking new questions, the biggest one being: Who can tell me more about Henrietta Childress, or for that matter, Etta Childs?

CHAPTER 2

WITH FRIENDS LIKE THESE...

The homicide office at the police department building was located a little too far for Sheen to walk to with any great convenience, so he chose to drive there in his 1948 maroon Ford Coupe. Climbing the stairs to the squad room on the third floor, he couldn't help but think of the sad metaphor that represented the reality of his failure to climb the proverbial stairs to the department's elite investigative division during his tenure with the City of Miami police.

His ascension in the ranks was stalled when the request to be transferred out of the vice squad, that he had earned with a guaranteed promotion, was blocked by the then new Lieutenant of Homicide. The feckless jackass, as Sheen called him, had chosen the open slot on his shift of murder police as an opportunity to promote his old partner to the job that Sheen felt should have been his. Not only did that incident permanently soil his opinion of the Lieutenant, but also caused him to reconsider working in a department that would so blatantly allow the higher-ups to bring their best buddies to the top of the ladder with them over more deserving detectives. Within the next three months Sheen put in his notice and left policing for the private investigation racket.

Sheen entered the homicide office and found the desk of his former vice squad partner Rupert Tierney. His ex-partner was as logical looking a man as one could find. A cop? No, one might say if they came across him. A literature professor at Oxford, maybe. He just had that appearance... the glasses perched just beneath the bridge of his nose, a set of peering eyes always looking to find the reasoning behind anything and everything he encountered. Even a receding hairline that gave him a mature, contemplative outward show.

"As former partners go, you aren't much for staying in touch with your old pal, are you?" Sheen asked.

Tierney looked up and glanced at Benjamin with a smirk that hinted he still enjoyed his former colleague's badgering. "Is that good or bad?" asked the homicide detective.

"I don't know. I haven't had many former partners."

The old friends shook hands and exchanged grins. "How are you, Benny?" Tierney asked.

"Doing all right, I guess. This racket treating you okay?"

"About the same as ever."

"That bad, huh?"

Tierney chuckled as he gestured to the empty chair in front of his desk, which Sheen gratefully accepted with a nod of the head as he sat. "What about you?" Tierney asked. "How's the nine to five on your end?"

Sheen casually raised his shoulders in a non-committal shrug, "Enough money's in my pocket, so what right do I got to complain?"

"Sure, sure. But why the surprise visit?"

Sheen tried to pass things off as good naturedly as possible when he replied, "What? A guy can't just come in and say hello to his pals?"

"Certainly. Guys do all the time... Only not you. Benjamin Sheen who left the department with a sour taste in his mouth isn't exactly the Christmas card sending type, so what's the reason you're here? You want something, I just want to know what it is."

Sheen knew he couldn't play it coy and decided to come right out with it. "Etta Childs," he said bluntly.

"Colored actress," Tierney responded. "Died a few months ago."

"*Murdered* a few months ago," Sheen corrected him.

"Right. So, what's the point?"

"You caught the case, I wanna know what you found."

"Why?"

Sheen's shrug again showed his disinterest in complicating matters. He just wanted the answers to his questions quick and easy, old pals or not. But clearly he could see that Tierney wasn't going to cooperate without full disclosure so Sheen went further into detail. "Her brother," Sheen confessed. "He came to my office, asking if I could look into it."

Tierney scoffed at the notion, not appreciating that his official investigation was now being surpassed by an outside party, but also bothered by the incredulity of this uppity black fellow to seek alternate sources of detection. "Wendell, right," Tierney confirmed. "What you mean to say is he hired you to investigate, not he asked you to look into it."

"That's the general idea, yes."

"Unbelievable." Tierney mulled it over, whether or not to put his pride out of the way to help his friend. True, he didn't like the thought of this dead movie star's brother taking matters into his own hands and seeking out the assistance of a private investigator, but none of that was Sheen's fault. After reasoning it out for a few moments, Tierney complied. "What do you want to know?"

"Whatever you can tell me."

"Etta Childs, real name Henrietta Childress, was strangled in a home that she owned in Brownsville."

"Strangled with what?"

"Best we can tell, no implements were used. Seems the killer throttled her with their hands."

"Any suspects?"

Tierney didn't even bother with words, he just let a solemn shake of his head express the fact that he was nowhere with the case.

"Detective Sheen, that is... former Detective Sheen."

Sheen turned around to see who had made that impolite statement with such reprehensible gusto. Of course it would be him... the feckless jackass. Lt. Granville was incapable of walking through a room without seeming pompous and inept. Sheen had always felt it took a certain level of talent to live with both characteristics. It had been his experience that these flaws in humanity tended to be coupled in politicians, lawyers, some doctors and most criminals. Still after all these years it amazed Sheen that Granville had been made a Lieutenant. His particular brand of uselessness and arrogance was reserved for men who would be made captains and colonels of the police force, and definitely commissioners. But lieutenants and sergeants had to do actual police work, leading their squads and managing their detectives with a certain level of appreciation. So how the hell was a man like Granville ever supposed to do the job that required the unequivocal attribute needed for this vocation: to be real police. And also to be good at it.

"And what brings you out of that hole in the wall you call an office today?" the prick asked with enough sarcasm to fill the entire four story police building.

"Not much. Just stopping by to see what you've done with the place," Sheen said, equaling the bastard's sarcasm jab for jab. "I'm pleased to see it's still standing."

Granville eyed Detective Tierney as he directly stated, "I'm just surprised we haven't had more cases solved in this squad."

"Well, you really shouldn't be, Lieutenant," Sheen responded, happy to come to the defense of his old running mate. "I've always said you were a lead by example kind of guy."

Granville darted a look at Sheen with his beady, brown eyes. They were his only menacing feature as his face was a cross between Roscoe Arbuckle and your Uncle Joe, and his gut hung over his trousers in a way that made one question the physical fitness requirements of the department.

"Maybe if you didn't have such a damn smart mouth all the time, you might have gotten that transfer to Homicide, Sheen," the fat man said with contempt.

Sheen pretended to give it a moment's consideration before responding, "Somehow I don't think so... " he waited longer than usual to finish it with, "Sir."

"I know your business, Sheen. You better not be here asking about some case one of your deadbeat clients is mixed up enough to pay you for. No information leaves this office without my say so." Granville turned his attention to Detective Tierney, "You got that, detective?"

"Of course, sir," Tierney responded, hiding any nervousness of crossing his superior.

Sheen reassured the irritable frump, "Not to worry, Lieutenant. I've got Sun Sox tickets for Saturday, I wanted to invite Rupert along. Simple as that."

Granville shot one last look Sheen's way, then moved along to his office. He slammed the door behind him like a petulant child. Sheen thought: This guy's a leader of men in the squad room? Thank God I jumped ship when I did.

Tierney leaned in closer to Sheen and said, an apology already suppressing any joy in his eyes, "Listen, Benny... I can't help you on this one. Granville's on my tail for a few things. He's on everybody's tail, that's just the squad right now. Hell, it's the department!"

Sheen angled his head to gesture towards the door and said, "Walk me out."

Both men stood and walked towards double doors that separated the homicide squad from the rest of the police department. "Three months, I'm sure this thing feels stone cold by now. But you really haven't got anything for me? No suspects, fine. Tell me who you interviewed at least."

Tierney shook his head, "Can't do it."

"Well what the hell happened? Just tell me that. Did you hit a wall on this?"

"The investigation was set aside."

"What for?"

"Not what, who. Carol Wilby. Fourteen year-old girl and her mother. I'm sure you read about it in the papers. Murdered in their neighborhood."

Sheen nodded, familiar enough with the story. "Coral Gables."

"Uptown problems, downtown problems. You know what I mean," Tierney confessed truthfully.

Defeated, Sheen slowly nodded his head with a scowl on his face. "I suppose it would be pointless to ask for a peek at the case file."

"If Granville found out, it would be my badge. I know it."

"I understand."

"If you actually do get Sun Sox tickets, let me know."

"Sure, kid."

Sheen patted his old partner on the shoulder and opened the door to leave. He feigned a curious expression as he studied the door. "Huh. Seems as if someone has stolen your sign."

"What sign?" Tierney asked.

"The one that reads: Whites Only."

Sheen walked away, letting the door swing shut behind him. Tierney sighed his annoyance at the implication.

CHAPTER 3

CORNED BEEF AND SCRAMBLED EGGS

Snoring wasn't something that Sheen did frequently, but on occasion he would sleep so soundly that his involuntary nocturnal reflexes would appear. This particular morning he nearly startled himself awake, quickly choking back the last of his nasal sounds of repose and lifting his head up from the pillow. He used the back of his hand to wipe away a slight trace of drool that had formed at the corner of his mouth and trickled down during his rest. He was lying on his back, something that surprised him, as he generally tended to sleep on his side. Strange he thought, why did I sleep so well? Sheen typically slept poorly during a case, often finding his mind would race too much to get a good start on the sandman's visit. What was so different about this case? Why was his usual level of concern not keeping him awake until the wee small hours? Could it be that he had absolutely nothing on it thus far? Sheen wasn't convinced. If anything, that would give him more cause to lose his thirty winks.

Day two of the Etta Childs investigation and Sheen didn't quite know where to begin. Getting up would be a good start, so he figured he ought to sit up and greet the morning. As Sheen sat on the edge of his bed, cracking his back with a big, arching stretch, he heard the canine yawn of his three year old bull terrier, Doyle. Doyle was mostly brown, with white patches and a big grey swatch of fur that half-circled his left eye. Though clearly a bull terrier, Sheen figured that Doyle must be some kind of a mutt as his coat was too peculiar.

Sheen reached for the pack of Camel cigarettes on his night-stand and shook it. Nothing emerged. Sheen sighed with dis-appointment as he peered into the vast emptiness of a pack of cigarettes that had nothing but a couple remains of rogue tobac-co leaves. "Why would I have kept this?" Sheen asked himself. Doyle looked up, hearing the sound of his master's voice, but soon displayed his indifference to the detective talking to himself by licking his lips and pushing an exasperated breath through his nostrils.

Sheen stood up and walked through the house towards the bathroom. Dutifully, the bull terrier followed and found his master standing over the toilet bowl, relieving himself with a steady, plenti-ful flow of urine. After flushing the toilet, Sheen filled the sink with water, quickly lathered up some cream for a shave, and slowly ran a straight-edge blade across his face. As part of daily ritual, Doyle sat obediently on the floor, looking up at Sheen as he shaved, washed his face and dried it off.

The detective entered the kitchen with his trusty pet behind him. Sheen opened the refrigerator and the bread box, retrieving two slic-es of rye bread, mayonnaise, ham and Swiss cheese. He spread a thin layer of mayonnaise on one side of the bread, then placed a slice of cheese bookended by two slices of ham on the fresh rye. He looked down at Doyle, watching on with great interest. Sheen opened the vegetable drawer and peeled a piece off of a head of lettuce. He fin-ished constructing the sandwich and reached into the cupboard for a box, out of which he grabbed three shortbread cookies. He placed the sandwich and the cookies in a ceramic bowl on the floor. He poured about a cup of milk out of a carton into the bowl and stepped away. Doyle buried his face in the bowl and feasted on his breakfast. Moments later, Sheen walked passed him, dressed for the day and took his fedora from the hat rack. "I'm off to work, pal. See you tonight." Doyle barely raised his eyes in response as he devoured the meal in front of him.

⋏ ⋏ ⋏

Sheen sat at the counter of the "Nickel Dime" coffee shop on 1st street, just across from the courthouse and a few blocks away from his office. He watched as Doris, the waitress who still looked fetching in her early fifties, mostly due to her glowing eyes, poured his coffee. She had a voluptuous body that she had managed to keep from sagging into plumpness midway through life. In fact there had been a few nights over the years when, met with no other social engagements, Sheen and his breakfast server had used the convenience of his nearby office for romantic endeavors of a purely sexual nature. One night Mrs. Skeffington had left her purse behind and nearly fainted when she walked in on the sight of Doris, her hands clutched around the hat rack as she was bent over in front of Detective Sheen, enjoying a shared rhythmic thrust. After that, Mrs. Skeffington not only refused to ever step foot into the "Nickel Dime" coffee shop again, but took to spending hours each week thoroughly cleaning the outer office of the detective agency.

"A pack of camels too, Doris," Sheen said with his not quite awake expression.

Doris reached behind the counter and handed a pack of smokes to Sheen who quickly opened them and lit his first of the day. "The usual?" asked Doris, "Scrambled eggs, burnt toast?"

Sheen nodded as he slowly exhaled the smoke through a tiny "o" he had formed with his bottom lip.

"We've got corned beef hash today if you want to add it. Only eighty cents extra."

Sheen thought about it and felt like he would enjoy the breakfast special of the day. "Yeah, all right."

"You got it, sugar." Doris turned her head towards the narrow opening in the wall behind her and shouted, "Special with two scrambled, toast black!"

Doris nudged an ashtray in Sheen's direction which he tapped at with his cigarette, causing the gray mass of powder at the end of it to give way to a bright orange glow. The door to the establishment opened and Sheen tilted his head, raising an eyebrow as he heard the phrase, "Top of the morning, love," uttered at Doris. She smiled her pleasant grin at a fit gentleman with a large chest, stronger than average biceps and a pencil thin mustache. His eyes were a deep, dark brown and his smile was an instant charm. He turned to look at Sheen and barely got out the words "Good morning to you" before two men who had been sitting in the corner booth drinking coffee lunged at the new arrival.

The mustached rogue battled them off as best as he could. In fact he did surprisingly well against two guys who'd gotten the jump on him. Mr. pencil thin facial hair kicked one of the men back, almost like an upside down mule might have the reflex to do, sending the attacker crashing onto the booth's table. Coffee spilled onto the floor and silverware crashed to the ground. Fortunately for Doris the water glasses and coffee cups were spared any real damage. The other man involved in the fray reached back and punched the victim on the side of the face. This caused the dapper gent to drop, face first onto the counter next to Sheen. The fellow looked over at the detective and suggested, "Step in and help any time, pal."

Benjamin shrugged as he took another sip of coffee and flicked another ash from his cigarette into the tray. The attacker grabbed his opponent from behind, reaching to pull him up. But the man on the counter reacted with a reverse head butt, the top of his skull meeting his assailant's nose. The man yelped in pain as he grabbed his bloodied nose. The mustached charmer took a few steps backward, temporarily forgetting that there were two challengers and by now the man who had gone sailing onto the table was upright. He gave his victim a tremendous shove, knocking the gentleman back, off his feet and onto the floor.

"You owe Jimmy Dell, buster! It's time you ought to have paid," screamed the man covering his busted nose with a bloody handkerchief.

"How much?" Sheen asked.

"This don't concern you, mister," said the bloody-nosed goon's partner.

The debtor gingerly got to his feet, wincing as he put a hand on his abdomen. "Twenty-five dollars."

No sooner than Sheen had registered the information in his brain did he reach into his wallet and pull out two ten dollar bills and a five spot. He handed it to the guy with the busted face.

"No. He owes, he pays," the villain exclaimed.

"What's the difference?" Sheen asked. "It's a gift from me to him, he owes you the money, now I'm giving it to you."

The injured shylock considered it for a moment, then reached out and grabbed the bills out of Sheen's hand. "And what's your name?" he asked.

Sheen looked at him, very direct and responded, "My name's not important. You got what you wanted, now get the hell out of here."

The two thugs backed out of the diner and the bloodied leader glared at his adversary and ordered, "Stay out of the stone crabber's joint, wiseass." And with that they were gone.

Sheen picked up his cup of coffee and had another sip as the man sat at the barstool next to him. "Stone crabber's joint?" Sheen asked. "I thought you weren't playing poker there anymore."

The man smiled and replied, "I wasn't. At least, not until I learned that Warren Mackendrick was back in town... I just couldn't help myself."

"You take him down?"

Painful to think about, his smile was more of a wince as he recalled it, "Nah. I had three queens and he turns over three aces. What are the odds of set over set, you know?"

"It never fails, Mickey. You always find a way to open the door to trouble."

"True. But what can you do when trouble keeps knocking?"

Mickey Wails fancied himself a pseudo-Englishman. His parents were both British, one from London and the other from Manchester. They had crossed the pond when Mickey was in his early teens and he'd spent enough time growing from adolescence to manhood in America to lose his English accent. Though on occasion, particularly in moments of duress... or when he was drunk, traces of his accent would come out. His hair was naturally brown, but it appeared black with all the grease he used to shape it. And he wore it longer than most men did, making him resemble more of a teenage hood than the thirty-eight year old man he was.

To call Mickey a gambler would deny his many other "talents". He was a historian, incredibly erudite. He had also been a published writer of poetry and short stories. He was a sometime painter and even philosopher. On top of that he was quite the pugilist. He would fight from time to time, when he needed the money and there was an opening on a small card. Every once in a while Chris Dundee at the 5th street gym on Miami Beach would throw a few bucks Mickey's way to spar with some up and coming fighter. Among his other areas of expertise: Auto mechanic, chef, photographer, illusionist and claimed that, for a short time, he had been a gigolo. He also knew his way around horses. Sheen thought, you could call Mickey a renaissance man, but ultimately believed that would be an insult to the true renaissance men.

But probably his best ability was in seeking out and finding information. Mickey had been in the intelligence division during the war. Prior to his career as an unemployed jack of all trades, Mickey, then Michael Wellington, had been a Rhodes Scholar, ultimately leading to his military position during the second world war. Though Sheen and Mickey's paths had never crossed as soldiers in the European theater, their military experiences were one of the things they found they had in common when they met at Hannigan's Bar in 1947.

"Damn it, Mickey! Look what you've done to my floor," Doris fumed.

"Nothing's broken. Don't worry, love. I'll clean it for you," Mickey responded with charm and a hint of guilt in his eyes. He stood and headed towards the mess on the floor.

"No! Just sit there and try not to... touch anything."

"Very well," Mickey said as he resumed his spot at the counter. The bell at the kitchen window dinged. Doris turned around and placed Sheen's breakfast in front of him. Sheen reached for his fork and shoveled a forkful of hash into his mouth.

"Mmmm. That looks good," Mickey stated with eager eyes.

Sheen glared at Mickey, then relented. He pointed at his friend and instructed Doris, "One for him too."

Mickey smiled, appreciatively. "Thank you, Ben."

"Listen, that twenty-five bucks isn't a loan, it isn't a handout neither. I have a new case I'm looking into and I could use your help."

"Oh, I'd be happy to. What's the story?"

"Colored gal named Etta Childs was murdered a few months back, now the inquiry has found its way to my office."

"Etta Childs! I knew her... I mean, I knew of her. Seen her movies."

"Yeah well so far it's a big question mark, I don't have much to go on yet. Her brother hired me and he's gonna come up with some names to look at. Until he does, I'm gonna research the news angle. See what the write-ups were when it happened."

"Good idea."

"You, on the other hand, I want you to check out the people on the street. See if anybody knows something. Now she had a place in Brownsville, you should look there. She was a well-to-do Negro, so I'm guessing she spent some time in Overtown. Find out what you can for starters, then let me know."

"I'm on it."

CHAPTER 4

THE MAN WHO PUT PEN TO PAPER

Sheen sat on a stiff park bench, three planks of wood slapped onto a couple of slabs of concrete for support, with a backing of equal design. He lit up a Camel and patiently smoked it as he sat and watched a gentle breeze move through the trees at Bayfront Park, just off of Biscayne Boulevard.

He was waiting for the main branch of the public library to open for the day and he had arrived eight minutes before they would unlock their doors and let the literature patrons enter. When the doors finally opened, he took one final drag off his cigarette before butting it on the bottom of his shoe heel and tossing the extinguished Camel into a public waste basket.

As Sheen entered the building, which was little more than a year old, he walked past the bookshelves of popular literature and went directly to the periodicals section where he approached the librarian at the help desk.

"Good morning, sir," said the conservatively dressed woman in her early forties. "How may I help you?"

Sheen smiled and replied, "Yes, I'm looking for copies of the Miami Herald and the Miami News from about three months ago.

Is that something you would still have in the filing cabinets back there?"

"Well," she angled her head in thought, "They may be in the cabinets. It all depends on how quickly we have been able to convert them. Usually three to four months back, you'll have to check the micro-cards. But let's see how lucky you get."

She waved him back towards the wall of standing cabinets. "Come with me."

"Thank you, ma'am."

Sheen was in luck as copies of both local newspapers were in the file cabinet going back to the beginning of February, 1952. The February 20th edition of the Herald had a single paragraph about Etta Childs' death, but didn't go into much detail of it being a murder. There was brief mention of her having worked in the pictures, but it was mostly just a glorified obituary.

The Miami News, however, had several articles that month about Etta and her murder. The stories had been written by a man named Josh Riley.

February 19, 1952
LOCAL STAR TURNED MOVIE ACTRESS SLAIN
In the early morning hours of February 19th a caravan of vehicles from the police department, including the homicide squad, parked outside a residence in Brownsville. The cause for the commotion was the dead body of Negro movie star Etta Childs, discovered by her maid. Childs was found on her kitchen floor, apparently strangled.
Childs, 33, was an actress and singer who got her professional career off to a start performing at The Clover Club in Overtown. She also starred in various stage productions, including a Lyric Theater production of "Porgy and Bess". Eventually her success and word of her talent spread and she was cast as a singer in the 1949 film "Matinees

and Melodies". A number of other major motion picture roles followed, such as "The Lady on the Balcony" and "Broadway Belles", as well as the lesser known "First Train Out".

Police do not yet know who is responsible for Childs' murder, or how she was strangled, but their investigation has just begun.

The second article from The Miami News, also written by Riley, was published a couple weeks later in the March 6th edition. Written mainly as a follow-up piece, the author described the details of the case further than he had in the initial report. Since the homicide detectives didn't have much to go on, these details were still limited. One point the article mentioned was that the police suspected that Ms. Childs knew her killer. This conclusion was reached based on the signs of struggle only being in the kitchen, nothing to indicate otherwise anywhere else in the house, including the front entrance. Riley possibly overstepped his bounds as a journalist in the piece when he editorialized a bit stating "the fact that this case has stalled raises the question, is it just for lack of evidence? Furthermore, if this were June Allyson or Katherine Hepburn, would the uproar be more grand?"

Sheen thought about that last statement, and while he didn't necessarily disagree with it, he felt Riley had jumped the gun a bit too soon, only two and a half weeks after the killing, to assume that the police simply weren't trying hard enough. Then he remembered what Rupert had told him about the Childs case being stuck in a drawer for a while as the department investigated the Wilby killings. The more that thought circled around in his mind, the more he was convinced to call Josh Riley at The Miami News and ask if the writer had more information than what he disclosed in his story.

When Sheen arrived at his office building, the first floor was more crowded than usual. The ground floor was an emporium and a number of jewelers had set up shops and stands all along the lobby. On the way to the elevators Sheen had to cut through a decent sized crowd that were there for Kershings' "Summer Sun Sale", as it had been advertised over the weekend.

Once Sheen got to the office he sat behind his desk and placed a call to The Miami News. He was surprised to hear from the receptionist on the other end of the line that Josh Riley was no longer employed by the paper.

"Huh," Sheen bemused as he asked, "Well, do you know where he's working now? Or at least where I can find him?"

⅄ ⅄ ⅄

Josh Riley had not spent his entire career at The Miami News, or as a journalist for that matter. After graduating from Northwestern University, where he studied literature and theater arts, Riley had success very early. He wrote two plays, both of which were performed on Broadway, and the second of which won the New York Drama Critics Circle Award. An offer came from Hollywood to adapt his stage play for the screen and Riley jumped at the chance. His first screenplay credit was a success and kept him steadily employed in the movie business for the next six years. Though the money was coming in, Riley had seriously begun to dislike the industry in which he labored. In the spring of 1948 he decided to leave the business, dissatisfied and uninspired. When later asked what it was like to write for the pictures Josh would reply, "You have to learn to be a good whore."

Convinced he didn't want to return to the stage and feeling that Hollywood had sucked the desire to create fiction out of him, Riley chose to turn to the world of reporting. His first works as a journalist were all freelance. Starting in Los Angeles, driving cross-country, which had always been a desire of his, stopping in a few towns along the way to get paid for his stories, he ultimately landed in Miami, Florida. It would only be a few weeks before he was hired full-time by The Miami News in September of 1948.

Nearly four years later, in March of '52, Riley was shocked to receive a particular phone call. Josh sat in the newsroom, his fingers swiftly and melodically clacking the keys on his black Royal Quiet Deluxe typewriter, a portable model that fit into it's convenient carrying case. Josh took a momentary pause from typing to read over the words he had printed onto the page. His piercing, green eyes stared, sunken under his furrowed brow. He was thirty-five years old and starting to get love handles on his once fit frame. He brushed an open-fingered hand through his thinning hair, resting his elbow on his desk. He closed his eyes, just a moment's rest before deadline for the evening edition was to be published. "Okay, it's there," he thought.

"Copy!"

A younger, freckle-faced man who was just getting the start on his career rushed over to Josh's desk. Riley handed the young man the paper that he had just yanked out of the typewriter's carriage and watched as the unseasoned go-getter carried it over to the editor's office. Riley sat back, stretched his arms over his head and let out a gratifying sigh.

He vaguely heard the telephone ring on the other side of the room. He didn't think much of it since the phone rang frequently in the newsroom. But he looked up when one of the secretaries called out, "Riley! Telephone!"

Riley walked the length of the newsroom to where the telephone was fastened to the wall. On the way he passed the desk of the paper's primary photographer, a middle-aged man whose gray was starting to crowd his natural blonde hair. "Spring training, Josh. My Dodgers are just a few, short hours away for the next month."

"Really, you're going to put yourself through that again this year?" Riley asked. "You were in mourning all winter from that Bobby Thomson homer."

"Guy got one lucky hit, that's all. This year we get back to the series and we take down the champs. Mark it down."

"Your bums ever beat the Yankees and I'll eat my hat."

The photographer dismissed Josh's skepticism with a wave of the hand.

"Hello. This is Josh Riley," he said as he reached the wall and placed the telephone receiver to his ear.

"Good afternoon, Mr. Riley," the voice coming through the earpiece said in its confident, raspy qualities. "This is Jensen Stone. I'm Governor Eldridge's Chief of Staff."

Riley's eyes widened, as curious as he was stunned. "Yes, sir. I know who you are. What can I do for you?"

"Well, I'm only in town today and I would like to meet with you, perhaps we can get some dinner. I have a proposal for you."

"Me?" Riley was no less confused now than he had been a moment ago when he answered the call.

"Yes. Are you free this evening?"

"Uh... oh, yes. Absolutely."

"Terrific. Listen, I'm staying across the street at the Alcazar. How about we meet in the lobby around six o'clock and we'll go from there."

"Great. Sure."

Later that evening as Riley sat, waiting in the magnificent lobby of the thirteen floor Hotel Alcazar, he heard the familiar "ding" that an elevator signal made as a car arrived, soon to open. Jensen Stone stepped out of the elevator, immaculately dressed, a smile of recognition creeping across a weathered face, punctuated by a sharp chin. He walked right over to Riley and extended his hand. As Riley shook hands with the Governor's Chief of Staff, he noticed the man, who was in his early fifties, had small, round and dark, but very direct eyes.

"Good to meet you, Mr. Riley," Stone said. "Thank you for coming."

"Please, call me Josh."

"Sure thing. Do you have some place nearby that you could recommend for supper?"

"I do, but... At the risk of seeming rude..."

"Not at all."

"What is this about?"

Stone smiled, he liked the upfront question. "I'm here to offer you a job, Josh. We're looking for a new speech writer, we typically take on extra people going into an election cycle, we want you to be one of those people."

Josh was surprised, and had no reaction other than his frozen expression of alarm. "I'm not quite sure if that reaction is good or not," Stone said.

Josh finally uttered, "Mr. Stone..."

"Jensen."

"Jensen. I'm flattered, really I am. But..."

"Why?"

"Yes, exactly. Why me?"

"We've seen your credentials, your work at the paper, your theater background. The picture shows too. That one you wrote about Theodore Roosevelt, the Governor really liked that picture."

"Thank you, sir. But..."

"Josh, you can turn me down right here and now before I've really had a chance to talk to you and both of us are on an empty stomach, or you can let me talk to you about our plans. Governor Eldridge wants to run a strong campaign, he thinks you will be an invaluable writer on our staff. Re-election is only a few months away, three years down the line, he's looking at the White House. Now you can be part of that, be part of this legacy. Or you can be some guy that made a bad decision once in a hotel lobby because he wouldn't sit down to a meal. Now, do you know a good place or not?"

⅄ ⅄ ⅄

Months after a detailed conversation at the Red Coach Grill on 14th and Biscayne, the phone rang on Josh Riley's desk at the State House.

"Hello," Riley answered.

"Yes, hello. This is Ben Sheen, I'm a private investigator in Miami, Florida. Is this Mr. Riley?"

"It is. What can I do for you?"

"You wrote a piece when you were still with The Miami News. In fact, you wrote two, on a murdered Negro actress named Etta Childs."

Riley's interest was piqued by the mention of the movie star's name. "Yes. Are you investigating that case?"

"I am. I wanted to know if you could tell me anything about it... perhaps something that didn't make it into the article?"

"I'd be happy to, but... unfortunately, most of what is in the article is all there was to tell from an investigative point-of-view."

"What about from another point-of-view?"

Riley sighed, thinking for a moment about the fact that he had wanted to know more about Etta's murder and wanted to see the case treated with some regard by local authorities. "Nothing more than... just personal opinion".

"Ah-huh. Which would be?" Sheen let the question linger, hoping Riley would offer some thoughts of his own.

"It always bothered me that the murder was never solved," Riley admitted.

"Why is that? Plenty of murders go unanswered."

"Certainly, but... " Riley didn't seem to have a clear retort. Sheen picked up on that and followed with another question. "Did you know Ms. Childs?"

"No. But, I used to work in the pictures. You have to understand... people who work in Hollywood, they share a strange bond. Even if you've never met someone, but they worked in the movies... It's like a shared understanding. Of being in that world. I don't know how to explain. It's not elitist, it's just common experiences and the like."

"I see where you're coming from."

"You do?"

"I can share a knowing look with a fella I never met, because he might have been dug in a trench somewhere in Europe."

"Yes. Though, I would never presume to compare working in Hollywood to being in the war. Not honestly."

"I take no offense, Mr. Riley. I'm the one who made the analogy."

"Where did you serve?"

"France and Belgium mostly, '44. But let's talk about your articles. In the second piece you wrote, you mentioned that the murder was not getting the attention it deserved. You even implied that if this was a white actress..."

Riley cut him off, "I remember what I wrote. Look, I worked in Hollywood and before that, the New York stage, with all different kinds of people. Many blacks. They're good people, most of them...

What I mean to say is I've met as many unsavory folks whose skin color happened to be white as I have people of any other kind. So when a woman is strangled to death, I don't think the effort given towards that investigation should vary under any circumstances."

Riley looked up to respond to a subtle knocking on his opened office door. Standing at the entrance was a handsome, athletic man with the physique fit to wear the uniform of a Boston Celtic, though he wore his suit and tie rather nicely. He was Jonah Fisk, a dirty blonde, light-brown eyed man with an intense stare perpetually on his face.

Riley covered the mouthpiece of the receiver and looked at Fisk with raised eyebrows. As quietly as possible, Fisk, who was the Governor's personal driver and head of the security detail, reminded Riley, "We've got that town hall meeting at Florida State."

"Yes. I'll be right there."

Fisk nodded and walked away. Riley returned his attention to his phone call. "Listen, Mr. Sheen. I'm in a bit of a hurry and I need to get going. Is there anything else you needed to ask me?"

"Well, I was hoping you had some more insight, but I guess you've told me everything."

"Yes. Sorry I couldn't be more help... Listen, if you do find out more about the murder, would you mind giving me a call? Just as someone who opened that can of worms, I'd like to know what happened."

"Sure."

"Thanks."

"One more thing... You didn't have another follow up article you wanted to write?"

"Not really. I didn't have anything else to go on and any follow up points I'd brought up in the second piece. Couple weeks after that I got the job working here."

"All right. Thank you, Mr. Riley."

"You're welcome."

Riley hung up the phone and rushed away from his desk, grabbing his suit jacket as he turned off the light and exited his office.

CHAPTER 5

CORNER PIECES OF THE PUZZLE

It was nearly 8:30 at night and the sun had set just an hour ago. Sheen drove his Ford Coupe along a road, passing one house after another that rested just off the North shore of the Miami River. He reached his two-room residence at 678 North Northwest River Drive and pulled into the driveway. He stepped out of the vehicle, approached the front door and found it odd that his mailbox was empty. He turned the key in the lock and opened the door.

As Sheen stepped inside the living room, he was immediately alarmed by the light cast across the dining table at the far side of the room, emanating from the kitchen on the left. He cautiously approached, reaching inside his jacket where he kept a .38 Colt automatic holstered on his side beneath his left arm. His concern was heightened when he heard a rustling in the kitchen. He raised the pistol and pointed it towards the old-fashioned, western saloon style swinging doors that were affixed to the walls on both sides of the kitchen entrance. They had been there when he bought the house and he decided to leave them up because he found them amusing. Slowly Sheen crept closer and announced himself, "All right look! Whoever you are, you had better step out of the kitchen carefully. I've got a .38 pointed at you and I will use it."

A familiar voice spoke from within the kitchen, "Okay. Well, all I've got is a butter knife. Just making a sandwich here."

"For God's sake, Mickey!" Sheen stepped towards the kitchen and swung open the saloon doors. "You startled the hell out of me."

"Sorry about that," Mickey said as he sliced a tomato and placed it on his cold cuts and bread. Sheen looked down at Doyle, sitting on the floor and watching the sandwich routine. "Well, you're no damn good, are you?" Sheen asked his faithful mutt.

Doyle merely rolled over, all four legs in the air, wanting a belly rub. To Doyle, this seemed a reasonable request. "Ah don't be too hard on the poor lad," Mickey exclaimed. "He knows me." Mickey tore a piece of ham off his slice and tossed it on the floor. Doyle quickly gobbled it up.

This wasn't the first time Mickey had done this. He would, on occasion arrive at Sheen's house, see that no one was home, and find a way inside anyway. Sheen had offered to give Mickey a spare key, but Mickey shrugged it off, saying he didn't need one. Sheen appreciated that Mickey would break-in without actually breaking anything. The detective liked to think of his pal as Cary Grant in that movie *Topper*, just randomly showing up.

"So," Sheen asked, "What brings you along?" Sheen opened the refrigerator and retrieved a pitcher of iced tea. He poured a glass as Mickey explained, "I've got some information for you. I figured you'd want to hear it as soon as possible."

"Okay. What's the story?"

人 人 人

Mickey had spent the day talking to a number of people and getting as much on Etta Childs as he could. Much of his time was used in Overtown, the popular neighborhood where black folks had much of their businesses and nightlife.

Quite a few of the people to whom Mickey showed Etta's picture would recognize her from the movies, but not know her personally. Others would have seen her around, including one soda jerk who had stepped outside the diner he worked at to catch a cool breeze. He told Mickey that he had often seen her "on the Avenue", the phrase that many blacks used to describe an evening of socializing on 2nd Avenue, the strip in Overtown they referred to as "Little Broadway".

Mickey was perfectly comfortable on this side of town and rarely got a sideways glance. He knew many of the black people around here. He had played in their backroom card games, and fought and trained with plenty of them at the gyms. Also, Mickey was just that kind of person who seemed to be welcome at any table. A man who was well-liked and widely considered to be a "Good Joe".

"Did you see what he did to Graziano? Knocked him out in the third round!" A tall, lanky black man with smudge marks of grease on his face and dressed in a gas station attendant's uniform recalled a recent middleweight championship bout. He spoke to a stocky black man, dressed in professional attire. "And that's just what Sugar Ray Robinson is gonna do to Joey Maxim at Yankee Stadium in a couple of weeks," said the mechanic.

"I believe you're right there."

Mickey smiled at the two men, "How are you gentlemen today?"

The mechanic shrugged, said he was okay. The businessman merely said hello. Mickey raised the picture of Etta Childs and asked, "Either of you know this lady?" Both men studied the photo and the mechanic stated, "That actress, ain't she? Wasn't she the one got killed a while back?"

"Yes," Mickey responded.

"Sure, but before that she was from 'round here," the business-man confirmed. Mickey looked at him and asked, "Did you know her?"

"Years ago. When she was younger, she used to work up at Clifford Dee's place."

"The Monarch Diner?"

"Yeah," said the mechanic. "You know it?"

"Sure. Listen, had either of you seen her around before she died?"

"Just to say hello to," replied the businessman. "She was real friendly-like. Even after all that movie glamour, she always knew where she came from. And she was proud of it. That's a rare thing in rich people."

"I thought you was rich people, Buster," quipped the mechanic.

The businessman chuckled and Mickey cracked a smile. The mechanic turned his attention towards Mickey and asked, "Why you askin' 'bout her anyhow?"

"I work with the detective agency that's investigating her murder. Just trying to get some background."

"Well good luck to you," the businessman offered.

Mickey had been in The Monarch plenty of times over the past few years and he was well acquainted with the proprietor, Clifford Dee. Well respected in the community, Clifford Dee was a deacon at his Baptist church and most of his actions in life were based on what he would call "goodly Christian ways". He was often known to give someone a job for the day, if they needed it. And had also, from time to time, let people have a hot meal even if they couldn't pay him till next week or so. Being a man in his sixties, his wisdom and experience in life was often sought after and Mr. Dee was something of an unofficial counselor to many of the folks of the neighborhood.

"Mr. Dee," Mickey said as he entered the diner.

"Bless my soul, Mickey Wails! How are you today?" Clifford Dee asked in his customary jovial way. Dee was a large man, both in height and around the waist. He wore a pair of glasses that seemed to disappear in his widely rounded face. He had a great laugh, that started as a wheeze and graduated to a guttural boom.

His diner was charmingly simple. A few booths, a couple of two seat tables and a high top bar with five stools. It was the kind of joint that had the grill right behind the counter and all the food preparation happened in view of the customers at the high top.

"I'm good, Mr. Dee," Mickey responded. "How are you?"

"Oh, I can't complain. What can I get for you?"

"Cup of coffee."

"Coffee. And Mrs. Dee has got homemade peach cobbler today and I will take it as a personal insult if you do not try some." Dee smiled and raised his eyebrows.

"Okay. Coffee and peach cobbler, then."

"Now you're talkin'." Dee poured a hot stream of coffee into a cup, partnered it with a saucer and slid it in front of Mickey. As he sliced a piece of cobbler and put it on a plate he asked, "What brings you by today?"

"I'm doing some work with a private investigator. He's looking into the case of Etta Childs."

"Mmmm. Awful things that happen." Dee handed Mickey a plate of cobbler. "Of course I know'd her when she was just Henrietta Childress, a little ol' thing serving breakfast to my customers. Sweetest young lady you'd ever meet."

"She ever come around after she'd been in Hollywood?"

"Oh my, yes. All the time. She had a house here, you know? Over in Brownsville. She didn't live here permanent, since all her work was out west. But every chance she got to come home, here she would be. Always comin' in here for breakfast."

"Would she be with other people?"

"Now and then. Old friends from the neighborhood. Mostly girls she growed up with."

"What about men? Was she dating anyone around here?"

Dee shrugged, "Few years ago, maybe. But recently, she did have a gentleman that she was seeing. I never met him, never saw them two together or nothin'. But she talked about him a few times. Her face would light up just like the sunshine talkin' 'bout him. Said his name was Nate."

"She describe him?"

"Not to his looks so much as his actions. How happy he made her, that sort of thing."

"It's a shame really."

With a puzzled expression Dee asked, "What's that?"

"That Mrs. Dee is already married. Because this cobbler is excellent."

Dee chuckled and let Mickey know he would pass his appreciation along to the wife. The mechanic who had been down the block earlier walked in and sat down next to Mickey.

"Afternoon, Woodrow," Dee said to the mechanic.

"Mr. Dee," he replied.

"You gonna have your usual sandwich?"

"No sir, not today. I'm needin' a big lunch now. Tow truck just brought in a fella's car and damned if it ain't a Oldsmobile. And nothin' can ruin my day like workin' on a Oldsmobile."

Dee laughed and asked what the mechanic wanted. "You got any of them pork chops you fry up?" Woodrow asked.

"Sure do."

"I'll take them."

"Greens and black-eyed peas?"

"Yes sir," the mechanic sat there, thinking to himself. "Rocket engine," he stated, bemused as he rolled his eyes and shook his head. "Got that pushrod engine. Whole lousy thing's a mess."

Clifford Dee served the mechanic a cup of coffee, then started frying his pork chops.

The mechanic took a sip of his coffee and turned towards Mickey. "Hey, Mr. Detective. I did think of somethin' 'bout that actress."

Mickey replied, "Yes?"

"There's a boy named Clete Tompkins, he's a young boxer from 'round the way. He was plenty interested in your movie star."

"How so?"

Dee listened over his shoulder to the conversation as he cooked. He chopped some red onion and garlic, then shifted the pork chops over to the side. He tossed some fresh collard greens, the onion and garlic onto the pork drippings on the grill and mixed it all up.

"Boy was sweet on her, I mean somethin' fierce. But that lady wasn't havin' none of it. I think she had a fella already."

"I remember that," Dee spoke up from beyond the counter. "They was friendly with each other, even sat down in here together a couple times. But that Tompkins boy wanted it to be somethin' more than that. Henrietta just wasn't interested on account that she was already seeing that other fella."

"This Nate guy," Mickey said.

"That's right."

Mickey asked the mechanic, "You say Clete Tompkins is a boxer?"

"Mm-hmm".

"He's a comer?"

"Yeah, he sure is."

"If he's a comer, he's probably working at the 5th street gym."

The mechanic nodded his head. Mickey extended his hand and said, "Thanks." The mechanic shook hands and responded, "No problem."

"What do I owe you, Mr. Dee?"

"Thirty cents."

Mickey dropped some change on the counter and headed out. "Thanks for the hospitality. See you around."

Mr. Dee waved a hand and said, "Any time." He brought a plate of fried pork chops, black-eyed peas and collard greens to the counter and placed it in front of the mechanic.

The mechanic looked down at his meal and shook his head. "Oldsmobiles."

⊥ ⊥ ⊥

The 5th Street Gym was located on the Southeast side of Miami Beach, off of Washington Avenue. Mickey walked in and was greeted by several boxers and employees with fond wishes and smiling faces. Mickey trained at the gym from time to time and sparred with some of the up and coming fighters that Chris Dundee was working with. Mickey approached a short old man who was nearly bald that was assisting a lean welterweight in removing his gloves. No one had ever known the old man's first name, he was simply referred to as McArdle as long as anyone could remember.

McArdle saw Mickey heading towards him and smiled, revealing a top row of teeth that were down to four or five, all spaced apart from each other. "Mickey Wails as I live and breathe," the aging corner man said.

"How are you, McArdle?" asked Mickey as he shook the man's hand.

"Things is good. You?"

"Keeping alive. Is Chris here?"

"Nah. He decided to take some time off."

"What about Angie?"

"He ain't around just now either. Somethin' I can help you with?"

"Just asking around. You know this Clete Tompkins kid?"

"Oh sure. He's been workin' here for the last seven, eight months."

Mickey nodded his head, interested to see what McArdle knew. "Tell me about the guy."

"He's got a good left, knows when to bring it out. Blocks just right, don't leave himself open too much. Needs some better stamina for the long rounds, but he's lookin' good. Lookin' real good."

"Tell me about him, not as a fighter. What's his story?"

"Seems like a good kid, very polite. He's got a mean streak in him though, but keeps it in the ring. I never saw him act cross with nobody if you take my meaning."

"I'm hearing he was interested in this actress."

"Yeah yeah, sure. Colored broad. Believe you me, if I was one of them, I'd be after her too."

Mickey smiled, amused by the old man's reaction to Etta's charms. "Nice looking girl, huh?"

"Oh boy," McArdle exclaimed as he quickly shook his hand back and forth in the air, as if Etta Childs was too hot to handle.

"Listen, how can I talk to Clete Tompkins? Is he around?"

"I gotta tell ya, Mickey. I don't know where the kid lives. But he's on the undercard tomorrow night at the auditorium."

"I see. Thanks, McArdle." Mickey shook hands and the older fellow said, "You're gettin' soft, Boy-o. Gonna have to get you back in that ring, see what's still kickin'." He smiled his mostly toothless grin as he watched a chuckling Mickey Wails walk out the door.

⋏ ⋏ ⋏

Mickey sat at Sheen's dining table, chewing on his sandwich as Sheen smoked a cigarette and sipped on his iced tea. Mickey swallowed his last bite and said, "So I figure we'll head down there tomorrow and talk to this Tompkins guy."

"We're just gonna get on this kid, start questioning him? Do you know how big he is?" asked Sheen.

Mickey replied, "He's just some palooka fighter. He's a pug, we'll brace him."

"You're just some palooka fighter."

"Yes, I know... But I got character."

Sheen smiled. Mickey added, "Oh, by the way. I brought your mail in for you." Mickey pointed to the envelopes on the table.

Sheen nodded, not so much concerned with his mail, but rather the vague details of this murder case. By his count they had a mysterious lover, an amorous fighter and a broadminded journalist. Would any of this lead anywhere? He stood up and grabbed the telephone receiver off the wall. He called Wendell Childress and asked, "Have you had the chance to write down those names?" Wendell said he had and Sheen agreed he would stop in at the 7th Street Diner in the morning.

Sheen hung up the phone and returned to the table with the inquisitive expression that his face would hold when he was deep in thought. He took one final drag of his cigarette, slowly exhaling the smoke as he smothered it in the ash tray, burnt down to the writing on the paper.

CHAPTER 6

SERENA

Sheen pulled his Coupe up to the curb on Northwest 3rd Avenue and 7th street and parked it in front of Wendell Childress' diner. Sheen stepped out of the vehicle and walked onto the sidewalk. A young Negro, maybe twenty-five glared at Sheen, half menacing, half surprised. Sheen was cautious not to fully retreat his eye contact, but not to linger. As he strolled closer to the front door of the diner, a much older black man, easily in his sixties walked by. As he passed the old-timer, Sheen nodded and tipped his cap, a gesture that at one time seemed unfathomable, and still was in some places.

Sheen entered the diner and was impressed with the look of the place. It was very nicely furnished, not basic by any means. Sheen figured this must be a hopping joint for Negroes out to dinner before or after a picture show, or a night at one of the clubs. A young waitress raised an eyebrow when she looked at Sheen before asking in her pleasant, high-pitched voice, "Sir? Somethin' I can help you with?"

Sheen replied, "I'm looking for Wendell Childress. Is he in?"

"Yes he is. I'll go get him."

"Thank you."

The waitress used the back of her hand to wipe the beads of sweat that had collected beneath her curly black hair onto her dark brown forehead. She walked past the counter towards the "employees only" doors that led into the kitchen. After she disappeared, Sheen moved towards the counter to take a seat. But something on the wall next to the kitchen doors caught his attention. Framed and on display was memorabilia and accolades from Wendell's service in the second world war. He had been part of the 92nd Infantry Division, 5th Army and had fought in the Battle of Monte Cassino. Sheen was studying the military history when Wendell stepped out from behind the kitchen doors.

"My sister put all that together for me," Wendell stated as he noticed Sheen looking over the display case.

Sheen turned his head and noticed Wendell standing there, looking fondly at the display with pride. "I didn't realize you had served," Sheen said.

"Yes indeed. '43 to '45, last year of that time in Italy."

Sheen nodded, admiring the display. "You in that war?" Wendell asked.

"Mm-hmm," Sheen said. "82nd Airborne."

"Normandy?"

Sheen nodded, "Belgium too, Germany at the end." Sheen pointed to the framed pieces and said, "Nice work. She do that before she went off to Hollywood?"

"Oh, no," Wendell responded. "This is my younger sister did these. I'm the middle child."

"I see."

Wendell indicated to the counter for Sheen to have a seat, an invitation that Sheen accepted.

"You got that list for me?" asked Sheen.

Wendell reached into his back pocket and produced a piece of folded paper. He unfolded it and handed it to Sheen. The investigator looked it over and immediately noticed that the list was only about twelve or so names long. Before reading through he asked, "Is Nate on here?"

Wendell looked at Sheen, puzzled. "Don't reckon I know a Nate. Who is he?"

"I was hoping you could tell me."

Wendell shrugged and just as he was to give it some thought, the tiny bell at the diner's entrance rang. Wendell looked towards the front of the diner and smiled as he saw a woman in her late twenties step in, the door closing behind her.

"Hey there," Wendell said. Sheen raised his eyes to see who was approaching and the rest of his head followed. He was stunned for a moment, surprised by his own reaction, but couldn't help the response he had to her presence. Her smile was glorious, a real thing of beauty and it lit up the room as she said hello to Wendell.

"Detective Sheen," Wendell introduced the woman, "This is my baby sister, Serena".

Sheen smiled and extended his hand, gently shaking hers. He felt a ridiculous warmth in his chest, something he found embarrassing and childish, as he held her cinnamon brown hand, her palm pressed against his. Her sister was a glamorous movie star, but in Sheen's opinion, Serena was the true beauty. Her eyes were a shade darker than Etta's and her smile less mysterious, rather comforting and sweet. She had that irresistible combination of cute and adorable mixed in with her beauty, something her sister was far too exotic looking to achieve. She was also more filled out than her sister when it came to her body. Etta Childs was very fit, not too skinny, but certainly not curvy. Serena, however, she was a woman with a gorgeous hourglass figure, curvy in all the places a man might like.

"It's nice to meet you," Serena said. Sheen even liked the sound of her voice, feminine enough but not too high-pitched or nasally.

"Yes..." he fumbled his response. "I mean, you too."

Sheen let go of the handshake. He couldn't believe he was actually nervous, but he was really quite taken with her. But the guilt of feeling this way made the moment bittersweet. He was a white man and nobody would agree with his visceral reaction... uptown, downtown or any town.

"Sesa, you know of a Nate that Henrietta knew?" Wendell had asked the question. Sheen thought to himself, Sesa? Is that what he called her? What does that mean? But he didn't wonder about it too much, still trying to get past his adoration for his client's sister and hoping that it didn't show.

"Nate," Serena thought. "Can't say that I do." She looked at Sheen and asked, "Why do you ask?"

"Just a name that came up," Sheen explained. "Seems like he was someone your sister was seeing, romantically."

"I can't help you there," Serena responded. "Henrietta didn't talk to me much about her relationships. Not with men, anyway."

"Then I guess you don't know anything about a Clete Tompkins either?"

Serena shook her head, never having heard the name before. She consulted with Wendell, "How about you? Do you know him?"

A look of irritation crawled across Wendell's face and through a grimace he spouted out the words, "Yeah, I know that guy. He'd been interested in Henrietta for a few months. Always followin' her around, puppy loved to tarnation. Didn't care much for him, to be truthful."

Serena shot a concerned expression Wendell's way and demanded, "How come you never told me this?" Sheen saw the look of concern on Serena's face and felt he was correct in reading it as being protective of her sister. Though it wasn't hard for Sheen to find any of Serena's qualities endearing at that moment, he appreciated her caring attitude towards Henrietta.

"I didn't want to give you no cause to worry like you always do," Wendell replied.

Sheen followed up with a question, "Why didn't you like this Tompkins character?"

"Boy's a boxer. I seen that kind," Wendell continued, "They get hit like punching bags, enough of that and they can act real crazy. Wasn't exactly what I wanted for my big sister."

Sheen nodded. He examined the list that Wendell had provided and asked, "Anything particular you can tell me about the names on this list?"

"Let me take a look," Serena interjected. She stepped in closer to see the paper Sheen had laid out in front of him. She placed a hand on the counter and her bent elbow was just barely touching Sheen's arm. Silly as the insignificant contact was, Sheen liked it. He began to ask the questions in his mind that all men ask when near an attractive woman: What would it be like...? The scenarios of all possibilities ran through his mind. How many of his curiosities were based on her being a black woman, he did not know. But he knew he enjoyed her company, especially standing that close to her.

Serena went over the list and Sheen wrote his notes as she spoke. Wendell occasionally chimed in with additional information of the people on the list. Most of them were friends and neighbors. Sheen recognized even then that the list seemed a bit futile. Based on the descriptions given by Etta's brother and sister, most of these names belonged to people who probably wouldn't harm Etta unless there was a motive driven by some deep, dark secret. Sheen would check these people out regardless, but his best lead still seemed to be this love-lorn boxer. Sheen proved as much when he told Wendell and Serena, "Tonight I'm going to talk to Clete Tompkins, see if I find anything."

Sheen stood up and assured them both, "I'll keep you up to date. Thanks very much for the names."

He smiled at Serena and said, "Ms. Childress."

She asked to be more casual when she offered, "Serena." Sheen liked the correction and grinned as he said, "Serena. A pleasure." He turned to look at Wendell and said, "Mr. Childress."

Sheen walked out of the diner and approached his vehicle. He folded the paper with the names and tucked it into his jacket pocket. He set all thoughts of Serena Childress aside to focus on her older sister and the question of her murder. A question he would certainly pose to Clete Tompkins.

CHAPTER 7

FIGHT NIGHT

The Miami Beach Municipal Auditorium was a two year old building on the Northwest corner of 17th Street and Washington Avenue. It was a performance venue that featured classical operas and ballets, as well as the latest popular entertainers like Frank Sinatra and Jackie Gleason. It was also the occasional venue for boxing matches. And on this night Clete Tompkins was fighting an accomplished middle-weight named Patrick Flannigan, a climber with a 16-3 record.

The maroon Coupe pulled to a stop at the curb, and Sheen and Mickey stepped out of the car and walked towards the auditorium. They stood at the rear entrance and Mickey pounded the pinky side of his fist against a steel door. A few moments later a rotund man with a heavily scarred face and an awkwardly bent nose opened the door. Looking at this guy's mug, Sheen pegged him as an ex-slugger hanging around the business though his days in the squared circle had long since passed.

"Hey, Mick," the doorman said with a smile as he looked at Sheen's partner.

"How's the world treating you? Making it okay?" Mickey asked.

"I'll live, one way or another. What's the story here?"

"Got any standing room inside for me and my pal?"

"Sure thing, Mick."

The big fella stepped aside and let Sheen and Mickey in the building, dutifully closing the steel door after them.

Mickey lead Sheen through the service corridors and hallways of the building. It was dead air, still. Mixed with the funk brought on by men drenched in perspiration that had circulated the halls and dressing rooms all night.

Another scent flew into Sheen's consciousness as he and Mickey entered the auditorium. Stale popcorn and cigar smoke. The place was loud with chatter that occasionally gave way to cheers and scattered instances of shouting directed at the two fighters in the ring. Sheen and Mickey stood at the back, just near the boxers entrance to the arena. They watched the Tompkins-Flannigan fight which, according to the large cards carried by a pretty girl between three minute intervals of the sweet science, was now in the third round.

Tompkins seemed to be ahead in the fight. Not that Sheen and Mickey knew anything about how the judges had called the first two rounds, but because they could tell that Flannigan had taken more punishment. The young Irishman had pronounced red marks on each of his temples and his right eye was swelling and on its way to being shut. Tompkins, on the other hand, didn't seem to have too much damage, save for a little redness on his left cheek.

McArdle was right about Tompkins, Mickey thought. The young pugilist protected his body well. Flannigan was struggling to connect on most of the swings he threw at Clete. And the young Negro fighter seemed to be in control of the battle with his opponent. Most of the third round was dominated by Tompkins' hooks to Flannigan's body. Clete had developed a rhythm that Flannigan had yet to figure out... a few shots to the body, followed by the left cross to the head. Just before the bell rang, Flannigan was knocked to his knees when an uppercut from Tompkins' left fist caught him on the jaw. The rules of the fight were such that Flannigan couldn't be saved by the bell, but the referee only got a seven count on him before he got back on his feet and stumbled towards his corner.

During the break, Sheen watched Tompkins, sitting in the corner. He was listening to his trainer and nodding his head, but his eyes were constantly focused on the boxer diagonally across from him. Tremendous determination was the first characteristic that Sheen noted about Clete Tompkins.

The timekeeper whacked the bell and the two fighters jumped back into the fray. For Patrick Flannigan, quickly returning to the bout was moot. Fifteen seconds into the fourth round Tompkins hit a couple of jabs, square on Flannigan's nose. To protect the head, Flannigan raised his gloves. Tompkins saw the opening and took it. Right cross, left hook, both to the body. Flannigan gasped, the wind knocked out of him and hunched over before collapsing on the canvas. Flannigan spent the entire ten count getting his breath back. Once he did, it was too late. Tompkins was the winner.

Tompkins didn't do much celebrating. He had won and won without much of a struggle. Yet the referee raised his arm in victory and Clete merely nodded his head in recognition of the crowd's approval before returning to his corner and quietly exiting the ring. Sheen made note of this demeanor, not sure if it was good sportsmanship, a tremendous lack of ego or simply boredom.

By the time Sheen and Mickey made their way back to the locker room, Tompkins' gloves were off, a cold washcloth wrapped around ice was placed against his left cheek and his corner man was packing Clete's gym bag.

"Hell of a fight, kid," Mickey stated as he smiled at the mildly damaged fighter.

"Thank you," Clete replied. He looked Mickey and Sheen over, curiosity being the least of his thoughts. "And you fellas? Who are you?"

"Ben Sheen. I'm a private investigator," Sheen offered. "This is my associate, Mickey Wails."

Half of a grin crept across Clete's face as he said, "Mickey Wails. One of Chris' guys. They always talkin' 'bout you at 5th Street."

"Yeah, I've done some scrapping," Mickey said with a proud smile.

"So," Tompkins continued, "What you guys want?"

"We're looking into Etta Childs' murder. We'd like to ask you a few questions," Sheen said in a straightforward manner.

Clete hung his head, a sigh escaped his chest and he tossed the ice-filled cloth aside. His corner man peered up and said, "You ought to keep that on there another ten minutes, kid."

Tompkins gave no reaction, lost for a moment in his own thoughts.

"We hear you knew her pretty well," Sheen added.

Tompkins looked at his corner man and angled his head towards the door. The message was understood as the corner man placed the gym bag on a nearby table and stepped out of the room. Clete turned his attention towards Sheen and pointedly asked, "You find out anything?"

Sheen shrugged and asked, "How do you mean?"

"New evidence, anything like that."

"Well, no. Nothing new yet. I'm just asking questions, seeing what we can find and where to look."

Another sigh, followed by a disappointed shake of the head, displayed Clete's frustration with this state of affairs. Sheen wasn't sure if it was instinct based on human nature or born out of an ex-cop's intuition, but at that moment he had mentally crossed Clete Tompkins off his list of potential suspects.

"She was beautiful! You know that?" Clete asked rhetorically. "I don't just mean 'cause she was in the pictures. I don't just mean how she looked. She was beautiful in every way."

"Word is you were sweet on her," Sheen said. "Maybe even asked her out a few times."

Tompkins nodded, "M-hmm. And she turned me down. She was already seeing somebody."

Mickey intervened, "But you didn't stop asking."

"Not at first," Clete responded. "I couldn't."

"This fella she was seeing," Sheen asked, even though he already knew the answer. "You know his name?"

"Nate," Clete said, the jealousy still fresh as the name leapt from his tongue.

"Last name?"

"Never did know his last name."

"How long had he been with Etta?"

"Can't say for sure. At least six months, maybe longer."

"If you weren't dating, what would you say the nature of your relationship was?"

"We was friends. Good friends. She liked being with me, talking to me. She said I was a good listener. I knew friends was all it would ever be and it hurt like hell, but I just wanted to spend time with her. I don't know if y'all can understand that."

"Sure," Mickey interjected. "I once knew this girl in New York... she was from Queens, but she worked at the library. I would walk her to the bus stop and wait with her damn near every day, just to chat with her a while."

Sheen gave Mickey a sideways glance, thinking: What the hell is Mickey talking about? Was that an honest moment of recollection, or just Mickey being Mickey, quick on his feet to invent a story to relate to this kid they were trying to get information out of? Either way, it was unsuspected sentimentality Sheen saw in his old friend.

Sheen pulled a folded piece of paper out of his pocket. He opened it to reveal the list of names Wendell had provided. He handed it over to Clete.

"Recognize any of these?" Sheen asked.

Clete looked at the names. "Yunetta Bryce is from Etta's church. They used to go to Georgette's every Sunday after service for tea."

"Georgette's?" Sheen asked.

"Yeah. It's over on 51st." Clete returned his attention to the list. "Rube Tannen was her manager. I don't know the rest."

Sheen followed up with the question, "Any reason you can think of for either of them to have killed Etta?"

"You kiddin', right?" asked Clete. Sheen shrugged.

"When there's almost nothing to go on," Sheen explained, "I've got to look at everything."

"Well Rube got no cause to hurt Etta since her career was really takin' off and he gets fat on that, right?" Clete continued, "And Ms. Bryce is a nice, church going lady. I never heard Etta talk about any kind of quarrel with her."

"Can you think of anyone else she might have had problems with?"

"No. Etta just wasn't the kind of person to..."

Sheen interrupted as he finished Clete's thought out loud, "To have any enemies. Yeah, that's what I keep hearing."

Clete gave Sheen a cold stare and quite frankly asked, "That so hard to believe?"

Sheen looked into Clete's eyes, not sure if there were racial implications to the question or just a broken-hearted man protecting the idea of the woman he admired. Sheen simply responded, "I suppose not." Sheen tried a different approach and asked, "What about fear? Was she afraid of somebody? Concerned for her safety, threatened? Anything of that sort?"

Clete thought about it and the moment he realized he had an answer to that question, Sheen knew it too. So did Mickey. The epiphany was etched on Clete's face.

"Tell me," Sheen said.

"I'm sure it's nothing," Clete responded.

"Let us decide that."

"No, because it's... She wasn't in danger, she wasn't threatened or anything like that. But, she did have to deal with this guy sometimes."

"What guy?"

"I don't know his name."

"Who is he?"

"He's a bookie. Etta would be talkin' about settlin' up with him on account of the Lady. She said she hated to go see this guy and..."

"Go on."

"Yeah, she said she was scared of him."

"Who's the Lady?" Mickey asked.

"Used to be a singer," Clete offered. "Real famous too, but she ain't been doin' so well. Has a room over at Georgette's and Etta would look in on her. Sometimes she would visit the Lady and later she would tell me that the Lady had lost at cards and now Etta would have to go see that bookie. And she said how much she hated to do that, because she didn't like that man."

"And that he scared her," Sheen confirmed.

Clete nodded his head.

Mickey and Sheen left Clete in the locker room and didn't bother to stay for the main event. Sheen dropped Mickey off at a lady friend's apartment and drove to The Gin Mill, a bar a few blocks north of his office.

Sitting alone, a half-full glass of Irish whiskey in front of him, Sheen contemplated Clete Tompkins. Earlier in the evening, Sheen had wondered about Clete's attitude during his victory. Now he had his answer... this was a young man who was in the worst kind of love imaginable, unrequited. His energy and killer instinct had been lost once Etta Childs had been strangled to death. Maybe even before that, when she denied his advances. Sheen didn't expect Clete Tompkins' boxing career to go much further. It had been KO'd by something more powerful than any haymaker or uppercut could ever be... passion for a woman.

Sheen took a sip of his whiskey and his thoughts immediately, and predictably, turned from Etta Childs to her sister Serena. Sheen was startled by how strong his reaction had been when he first saw her. And if he was truly honest with himself, he'd admit that her image was never completely gone from his consciousness in all the hours since then.

This was dangerous territory and he knew it. White men don't date black women. It just doesn't happen. And it can't. Those were the words that Sheen constantly forced upon his mind to ward off his desires. But the torture of his struggle was overcome by the pleasant image of Serena Childress and her smile. Her eyes. Her sweetness. Pleasant thoughts like these cannot be easily wiped away.

"Look what the cat dragged in," a familiarly despicable voice said. Sheen rolled his eyes as he turned ninety degrees on the barstool and saw the bulbous manifestation of smug evil, Homicide Lt. Granville, striking a match and lighting up a Chesterfield cigarette. Any images of pleasantry that Sheen was enjoying had now vanished.

"Straight from investigative skid row," Granville added.

"What can I do for you, Lieutenant?" Sheen pondered.

"I think I'd like you to stay out of police business."

"I don't work for the police."

"And nothing makes me prouder than that fact. But you know what I'm talking about. You've got a client, they've got you snooping into one of our investigations and I'm telling you to lay off."

"I'm a business man. You're gonna tell me what cases I can work privately? I don't think so, fat man. So just sit behind your desk and continue to screw up what used to be a good department."

Granville shot daggers with the look he gave Sheen. "Stand up, you lousy son of a bitch."

"If you think I'm gonna be dumb enough to take a swing at a police lieutenant, than you're drunker than I thought."

"I'm giving you a free pass, Sheen. You can do anything you want, no consequences. One time offer."

"Anything at all?"

"That's right."

"You really want to see the Irish in me?"

"I gave you the invite, didn't I?"

Sheen looked Granville over, awfully tempted to go to work on the smug son of a bitch. But he thought better of it, waved Granville off with a gesture of the hand and reached for another sip of whiskey.

"You're not worth the skin on my knuckles, you bum," Sheen admitted.

That was all Granville needed to take a swing. He caught Sheen on the right cheek with a solid punch. It sent Ben to the floor and Granville stood over him anticipating a retaliation.

Sheen rubbed his cheek, staggered to his feet and started to laugh. "I've had worse from broads who were rough in the sack," Sheen exclaimed.

Granville's face turned red and he lunged for Sheen. Though a touch inebriated, Ben was still nimble enough to dodge the lumbering attempt that was Granville's attack. By the time Granville positioned himself for another tackle, the bartender and two other patrons stepped in the middle of the skirmish.

"None of that garbage in here! You two wanna get tough with each other, do it outside in the alley," the bartender angrily shouted.

"Never mind that," Sheen responded as he put some cash on the bar. "I'm leaving anyhow."

Granville fumed as he watched Sheen leave.

On the way to his Coupe, Sheen spotted a 1950 Buick Roadmaster that he recognized as Lt. Granville's automobile. A devilish grin crept across Sheen's face as he knelt down behind the car, pulled his pocket knife from his trousers and used it to deflate both of Granville's rear tires. As he perpetrated the self-satisfying act, he commented to himself, "You said anything at all, you stupid bastard."

Sheen whistled "Keep Your Sunny Side Up" as he walked to his Ford Coupe, got in and drove away

.

CHAPTER 8

THE LADY AND THE SCHMUCK

Around mid-morning the next day, Detective Sheen fired up the engine of his Ford Coupe and piloted it towards Northwest 11th street, which eventually turned into 14th avenue. He'd take that to 20th street, which he'd drive on for quite a stretch. He reached to the center of the dash and turned on the first of four knobs. A crackle of static filled the air for a second and a half, finally giving way to a radio advertisement.

"Smooooooke a Lu-ucky," shouted the man on the radio in an exuberant sing-song of the simple jingle! "Lucky Strike cigarettes," the ad continued, "Enjoy your cigarette! If you're not happy with your present brand, and a thirty-eight city survey shows that millions are not, smoke Luckies!"

"Smoooooke a Lu-ucky!" The bellowing musical refrain again interjected, followed by the spokesman's continued speech. "You'll get the happy blending of perfect mildness and rich taste that fine to-bacco, and only fine tobacco, can give you. Remember, Lucky Strike means fine tobacco. So get complete smoking enjoyment. Be Happy, Go Lucky!"

The exclamation point to the ad was one final emphatic chorus of "Smoooooke a Lu-ucky!" The commercial didn't really persuade

Sheen to go out and buy a pack of Luckies. But it did subconsciously cause him to reach into his jacket pocket, pull out his pack of Camels and light one up.

The cigarette advertisement was followed by a commercial for professional wrestling matches on channel four. "Tonight! See NWA Champion Lou Thesz as he takes on Gorgeous George! Also in action, Antonino Rocca versus Zebra Kid!" Sheen raised his eyebrow, amused and perplexed as he wondered: Zebra Kid?

As Sheen turned north onto 27th Avenue, a news bulletin began. The report played a portion of Governor Eldridge's speech given recently at Florida State University. In his speech the Governor spoke about the importance of education and setting goals for one's productive life. He got a rousing ovation when he spoke the brilliant and inspiringly written line "A society is only as good as the people who believe in it. If our civic goal is to build a great state, than surely our personal goal should be to prepare our children, and our children's children, to prosper in it. I have seen, on this day in Tallahassee, what our children can do. We're going ahead. And the future is extraordinary!"

Sheen couldn't help but think that Josh Riley, former newspaperman and current speech writer, wrote that line for the Governor. The detective also acknowledged that the speech was a thinly veiled disguise for a campaign speech wherein Eldridge was basically saying: The state of Florida is prospering and will continue to do so and I'm the guy that did it so vote for me.

The news report also played a clip of Governor Eldridge talking about his plans to start development of a statewide turnpike, like the one they had in Pennsylvania. Eldridge believed it would increase tourism and help local economies, particularly with the ever-growing numbers of Northerners taking vacations to Miami, Fort Lauderdale and West Palm Beach.

Sheen took a right onto 50th street, then went left on 26th Avenue. He drove a couple of blocks until he reached the parking lot behind 2540 Northwest 51st street.

Georgette's Tea Room was a two-story, thirteen room house located in the colored section of town known as Brownsville. It was open to anyone who could let a room, but often its tenants were black celebrities. Typically performers who played shows at the luxury resorts and clubs on Miami Beach, but were not permitted to stay at those same hotels due to segregation laws.

Georgette's also functioned as a social gathering place for well-to-do members of Miami black society. And each and every Sunday, afternoon tea was held.

As Sheen approached the building, a number of ladies sat on the porch, enjoying pleasant conversation set to the constant sound of the creaking chairs they slowly rocked in. He tipped his hat to the women as he passed and entered the building.

Inside, a sizeable collection of ladies in their Sunday best were gathered at several dining tables. The chatter of their conversation echoed and combined to make one solid, sustained boom of noise, highlighted by the clinking of metal spoons against ceramic tea cups.

A middle-aged woman wearing a homemade dress with a pretty flower pattern approached Sheen and asked, "Yes? Can I help you?"

Sheen politely removed his hat and held the brim with both hands at his waist. "Yes, ma'am," he responded. "I believe you can. I'd like to speak to one of your guests. Is The Lady about?"

Sheen felt foolish uttering that phrase, not having a name to go on and just referring to her as The Lady. He anticipated that the response might be 'What Lady? There are plenty of ladies here'. He imagined, from that point, the conversation might veer into an unfortunate Abbott & Costello routine. Much to his pleasant surprise, the hostess knew who he was talking about. Ben could see it in her concerned expression before she answered.

"I don't know. Who are you?"

"Benjamin Sheen, I'm a private detective. I'm looking into the murder of Etta Childs, see, and I know she was friendly with The Lady and I would like to ask her a few things is all."

Nervous, yet contemplative, the woman looked at the stairwell towards the second floor, wondering if she should call on her tenant. She turned her attention back to Sheen and stated, "The Lady didn't come down to tea, so I 'spect she may be feelin' sickly. But I can find out if she's up to company."

"I would be much obliged, ma'am."

The woman nodded and instructed, "Wait here a moment."

"Thank you."

She stepped away and Sheen turned his attention to the ladies in the other room. A few noticed him, some smiled as he nodded their way, others looked away in indifference or animosity. He wondered at first if Ms. Yunetta Bryce was among the crowd, but then thought it best to try and focus on one acquaintance at a time.

When the woman in the flower dress returned she said, "The Lady tells me she is happy to speak with you now, detective."

"Thank you."

"Follow me."

Sheen walked towards the stairs as the hostess escorted him up and towards The Lady's room.

As he was guided through the door of the room, he noted the immaculate design of the place. Everything looked like it was of fine silk and brass. The Lady's quarters were indeed befitting someone of class.

The hostess said in her pleasant voice, "Lady, this is the man who asked to speak with you."

Sheen stepped further into the room and was presented to a woman in her late fifties, sitting up in her bed, back propped against a wall of pillows. The satin sheets that draped over her bed were pulled up just above her waist. Despite the obvious harshness brought on by hard-living, Sheen could see beneath it to find a beautiful woman, who must have been absolutely stunning in her younger days.

"Ma'am," Sheen said respectfully, "My name is Benjamin Sheen. I'm a private detective and I'm looking into the murder of Ms. Childs. I understand she was an acquaintance of yours?"

The Lady nodded and gestured to a chair near her bed. Sheen grabbed the chair and turned it towards The Lady, where he could take a seat facing her.

"Henrietta was such a darling girl," The Lady said. "A most glorious woman... a tremendous talent. She was as kind to me as I can tell you. She told me how much she loved my singing and what my music meant to her. Oh my, that did my heart some good."

"Where did you meet Henrietta?"

"She had a room here at Georgette's for a time. This was years ago, of course. She was a good neighbor." The Lady smiled, fondly thinking back on those days. "Then she settled into a place of her own not far from here. But she would be here every Sunday afternoon, for tea. Unless of course she was out making a picture or performing somewhere else in the country." The Lady paused, not wanting her next thought to be remembered. "And then one Sunday... she just didn't show up to tea. We'd known she was in town, but..." The Lady's eyes went glossy and tears trickled over the bottom lids.

Sheen reached into his pocket for a handkerchief but The Lady waved him off with a gesture of her hand. She reached over to the nightstand by her bed and grabbed her own. Sheen noticed the uniquely designed handkerchief, embroidered with the letters "M.S.", was of very fine material which he presumed to be silk.

He noticed something else too. When The Lady reached to grab the cloth, her robe lifted off her wrist ever so slightly. It revealed an arm ravaged by needle marks. Sheen suddenly realized just what sickness The Lady had. It was an illness that many musicians of the time had caught, and the only relief from it was to feed more of the disease into the blood stream.

The Lady gently dabbed around her eyes, absorbing the tears and gently smiled, trying to recover quickly and resume conversation. "Such a tragedy. Young, lovely woman like Henrietta," The Lady said before flicking her tongue at the roof of her mouth, making a noise to comment on the shame of it. "And she'd been so happy, Detective."

"Is that so?"

"Oh my, yes. She'd met a gentleman who she was over the moon for. A well to do fella, always treated her so good. The way she talked about him... this was a woman in love. Believe me, I've seen them all my years. Was even one myself long ago, if you can believe that."

Sheen smiled pleasantly and said, "I have no trouble believing that, Miss."

The Lady smiled, "Oh and you're a charmer. How sweet. Thank you, Detective. You flatter me, but... The Lady is not the head turner she used to be. But there was a time on the avenue, when it was really jumpin' that I brought them in. Everybody wanted to see The Lady." The room practically lit up with the smile on The Lady's face as she thought on her glory days. In that moment, the look in her eyes was enough to make any man from eighteen to ninety-four want to get to know The Lady better. Sheen appreciated the simple moment of seeing her joy.

"Of course they still do very well, you know. They've got the shows, folks still go and have a night out in Overtown." Her smile turned to a coy look with a mischievous raised eyebrow and she said, "But not near as good as we used to."

"Ms. Childs was quite a performer I hear."

"Wonderful. Very talented, knew how to work that audience till they needed her on that stage same as they needed breathin'. The great ones is always like that. In fact, that's how Nate first saw her. On the stage at Copa City on Miami Beach. That man, like a lot of them, saw Henrietta and fell like a fool. Of course there's nothing foolish about love, and they were in love... but that's one thing that can sure have you actin' a fool."

The Lady got lost in her thoughts for a moment, and stared off across the room as she said, "All those men, nary a one not wantin' to catch her eye, dreamin' about Ms. Henrietta. But only one in the crowd that she saw and he's the one with her hand in his come the end of the night."

"Did you know Nate personally?"

"No, I never did meet him. But to hear her talk about him, that man must have been some kind of special. This was a girl with her head real tight and straight-like on her shoulders. But that man, she was lost in him."

Sheen nodded as he thought about how to carefully tread the path into the next topic. "Ma'am... I don't mean to be insensitive, honestly. But sometimes I have to ask questions because... well, such is the nature of my profession. I have no intention of embarrassing you. But, I need to ask... your relationship with Etta Childs... was there something she was helping you with that... ?"

The Lady's mood changed and the tone of the room became far more serious. "You want to know about the gambling," The Lady deduced.

"I apologize."

The Lady held a hand up, informing Sheen that the apology was not necessary, no matter how kind a gesture. She admitted, "Henrietta would often, when I wasn't feeling up to going, visit my bookie. There was times she paid my debts for me. I used to have fun playing cards, betting on horses... baseball games sometimes. But that went from having fun to needing those bets."

Sheen studied The Lady's face as she spoke and she was curious about the thoughts running through his mind. She felt she needed to explain, "Thirty-six years I been on stage. Every night, all over the world. Everybody clapping, smiling because of what I give them. That's a feeling can't nobody understand lest they been there. It's a rush of life in your soul that you never want to be without. Then one day the applause is gone... you want to replace it and you will try anything."

"This bookie, what's his name?"

"Thurlow Grayson".

"I hear that Etta may have been afraid of this man, is that possible?"

"Well, Henrietta was the kind of woman, I don't know that she'd ever been scared of anything or anyone in her life. But Grayson is an impatient man, I wouldn't be surprised if he used his strength against a woman if he had difficulty with her. Also, he's a white businessman and not many of those is kind to black folks."

"Where can I find him?"

"Runs him a pool hall out in South Miami. Just off South Dixie Highway, around 72nd."

"Thank you, Ma'am. You've been a great help to me."

"Detective, someone has to speak for Henrietta. I hope you know that."

"Yes, ma'am. I'll do what I can."

Sheen took The Lady's hand and kissed it as he stood and walked towards the door. He stopped and turned back to look in her direction when she said, "You know, they say it's terrible when the applause stops, but it's not true. Once the applause is smaller than it used to be, that's really the beginning of the end."

Driving home, Sheen thought about The Lady and her solitude, feeling like a woman who didn't belong in this world as it now existed. Sheen felt a sadness, realizing what she didn't, that she could still be a part of the world outside her own thoughts. Only she would have to accept her age and know that her beauty was not defined by how brightly her star had shined, or the youth she once possessed.

When Sheen returned home he called Mickey on the telephone and told him about Thurlow Grayson and his South Miami billiard joint. Mickey said he knew the place and offered to go talk to the guy. Sheen said that he'd had a long day and wasn't interested in thinking about it anymore for the night.

The welcome sight of Sheen's pillows at the top of his bed beckoned him. He dropped face first and in what seemed to be one, single motion in two seconds time, he entered his slumber.

$$\curlywedge \ \curlywedge \ \curlywedge$$

The next morning Sheen woke up and opened the closet by his front door and retrieved the leash that he kept Doyle on when they ventured out together. Sheen had a Monday morning ritual. He took Doyle out for a walk, three blocks down to Mr. and Mrs. Templeton's drug store. Sheen had always felt that Monday morning was automatically hectic for everyone, whether something on that particular day caused the stress or not. Sheen believed people were so prepared to dread Mondays that they woke up with the weight of the world on their shoulders. He firmly believed that it spread throughout the city and no one could have a pleasant commute no matter what they tried. Therefore, he refused to make any attempt to get to the office before nine-thirty.

Instead, he opted to walk Doyle to the drug store, stock up on Camel cigarettes and Hills Bros. coffee. He also liked to purchase a few sweet rolls that Mrs. Templeton usually made fresh on Monday mornings. They were glazed with a brown sugar and cinnamon filling and generally stayed warm and soft in the bag by the time Sheen would walk home.

This particular Monday, Sheen stepped out his front door to the alarming sight of an empty patch of grass where he had parked his Ford Coupe the night before. He stared at the unoccupied stretch of real estate, panicked by the sudden mystery. Doyle, too, knew something was wrong as he let out a couple of loud barks.

Sheen hurried to the end of his front yard, toes touching the road and looked in every direction. Then he ran into the house. He dropped Doyle's leash, but the trusty canine, sensing something was amiss ran in after his owner before Sheen slammed the front door.

Sheen reached for the phone, about to dial the emergency number for the police... then he changed his mind. He casually put the handset back onto the cradle of his black Western Electric bell rotary telephone as he finished reading the note affixed to his cupboard door.

The note read: "I've borrowed the car, Mickey."

Sheen let out a sigh of relief as he looked down at Doyle, grabbed his leash and walked from the house to the Templetons' drug store.

Twenty minutes later, when Sheen and Doyle returned, Sheen carrying a bag with two packs of cigarettes, a tin of coffee and a paper bag with two sweet rolls, the telephone was ringing.

Sheen placed his purchases on the dining table and answered the telephone, "Benjamin Sheen residence."

The voice on the other end was Mickey, catching his breath as he spoke, "Ben. You should get 'round here to U.S. 1 and 73rd. This Grayson character's here."

Sheen thought to himself: Where do I begin? He replied, "Mick... What the hell is going on?"

"I'm telling you, get on your horse and head out to 7241 South Dixie."

"You took my horse!"

"So borrow someone else's horse. Or get a cab."

"Mickey!" It was no use, he had already hung up. He looked down at Doyle, who had found a comfortable spot to lie down near Sheen's feet. Sheen said to the bull terrier, "You know that pal of yours is a real pain in the neck." Doyle stared up at the detective with no apparent response, perhaps not fully grasping the frustration of the incident.

Sheen dialed a number and reached into the paper bag, extracting a sweet roll from which he promptly took a bite. When Mrs. Skeffington answered the office telephone, Sheen quickly chewed and swallowed the pastry in his mouth.

He had apologetically asked Mrs. Skeffington to come to his house, pick him up and drive him to South Miami. On the way there she fussed at him for smoking too much, especially early in the day and for not having had a proper breakfast. Sheen's mother had long since been dead and his estranged wife was God knows where. He secretly thought to himself, did they really need to be replaced by my secretary?

Sheen gave Mrs. Skeffington the instructions to return to the office as he would drive back with Mickey in his own vehicle. She drove off and he headed towards the pool hall. Walking in that direction, he spotted the tail end of his Coupe parked around the side of the building. He moved towards it.

As Sheen approached the Coupe he saw Mickey sitting in the driver's side with the door open, his feet hanging out over the pavement and one shoe off. Mickey was removing one of his socks as Sheen walked up and said, "Thanks for the head's up, pal."

"No problem," Mickey said, not catching even a hint of the sarcasm in Sheen's statement.

"I'm kidding, Mick! You scared the hell out of me this morning. I thought my car had been stolen, I was just about to call the cops!"

"That's ridiculous, I left you a note."

"Yes, I know. I saw it after I ran back into the house in a state of panic. You know, you could have asked me to borrow it."

"I didn't want to wake you." Mickey draped his sock over his leg as he put his naked foot into his shoe and tied the lace.

"When it comes to taking my car, in the future, wake me. You're peculiar, I don't mind. But I don't need heart attacks first thing in the morning and... Why are you taking your sock off?"

"I talked to this guy already, nothing came of it. He gave me the brush, waved a little muscle my way. I figure if we're both here, we can handle him. I just want you to talk to him and I'll jump in."

"Okay, sure. That doesn't explain your sock though."

"Trust me." Mickey stood up and shut the car door.

"Says the man who steals my car."

Mickey handed the keys to Sheen and said, "There you go. Would a thief give you your keys back?"

Mickey and Sheen walked towards the building and went inside.

The place wasn't charming by any modern standards. All it needed was a little sawdust on the floor and it could have been a saloon in the old west. But it had plenty of booze, and some decent tables with tight corners and good felt.

Mickey gestured with his head towards the bar where a man sat with his back to the two investigators. Mickey whispered, "Go talk to him."

"That's Grayson?" Sheen asked. Mickey nodded, confirming.

Sheen followed with the question, "And what is it you'll be doing?"

Mickey shrugged the question off and gestured towards Grayson, nudging Sheen to go over to him. Sheen obliged and approached the bar. "Pardon me," he said. "Mr. Grayson?"

Thurlow Grayson, a pale man, almost albino, with wild curly hair that looked like it hadn't been combed in a month turned around to look at Sheen. Grayson's eyes were so sleepy, they nearly looked dead, and the lids were so close together they appeared almost shut. But the deep blue color shined through the tiny slots. He had no sculpted facial hair, rather a five o'clock shadow. And his flat nose did nothing to enhance his features.

"Yeah, what do you want?" Grayson asked. "'Cause I ain't open right now."

"I'm not here as a customer. My name's Sheen, I'm a detective."

"Cop?"

"No, private operator."

As Sheen spoke with Grayson, Mickey reached into one of the pool table pockets and retrieved two billiard balls. He dropped them into the sock he carried and twisted the sock around itself a few times.

"Somebody in here get roughed up or something?" Grayson asked. "'Cause it happens all the time, pal. Don't think I'll remember whoever you're asking for."

"No, this has to do with some of your other business interests."

Grayson stared Sheen down and said, "My other business interests? You may not be no cop, but you got that smart cop mouth. And it's fixin' to get popped."

Mickey slowly approached, unseen by Grayson or Sheen.

"Whatever you're into, I don't give a damn," Sheen stated assuredly. "It only concerns me in as much as my client's case. I just want to ask you a few questions about a woman you knew named Henrietta Childress."

"Oh yeah, the nigger girl that pays for the other one."

WHACK! Mickey swung the loaded sock and the two billiard balls smashed against Grayson's face. Startled by the action, Sheen watched Grayson drop to the floor.

"What was that?" Sheen asked.

Mickey answered, "I've already had a chat with him, he's not interested in cooperating. So we've got to rough the son of a bitch up."

Sheen and Mickey looked down at Grayson. He wasn't moving. Sheen nudged at Grayson's legs with his foot. Grayson didn't react.

"Jeez, Mick. You knocked him out cold."

Mickey stared at the unconscious man below them, shrugged and said, "Good shot."

"He can't answer questions if he's not awake!"

Mickey knelt down and placed two fingers beneath Grayson's nose. He felt the warm exhale and said, "Well at least we know he's breathing."

"Great. So you didn't kill him as part of your brilliant interrogation plan."

Mickey hopped onto the bar, reached behind the counter and grabbed the nozzle for the soda water. He aimed it at Grayson's face and sprayed.

Grayson shifted his body, shook his head and began to cough. Mickey stopped spraying and tossed the nozzle over the side of the bar.

Sheen pulled Grayson up so that he was sitting upright on the floor. Grayson immediately placed a comforting hand on his face. "You rotten bastards. What the hell did you do to me?"

"Listen, bookie. You've had dealings with Henrietta Childress and I want to know everything there is to know about that," Sheen said.

"Go to hell."

"Okay. You don't have to talk to me, but then my man's gonna show you what life is like collecting debts with only three fingers."

Grayson looked up at Mickey who was already giving him the hardass look.

"She had a friend, some old bitch used to be a singer. The old broad lost a lot of money and she owed me. This Childress woman comes to me and pays me when it's past due. Every time! Females or not, they were niggers late on their payment."

"You ever get rough with her?"

"Who? Childress or the old one?"

"Either!"

"I grabbed the old broad a couple times, let her know I was serious! I had to set an example, so she knows she can't just walk on me about her debt. I let some old black lady get away with that, what happens to my business?"

"So when did Childress start coming around?"

"Okay, so one time I guess I got pretty tough with the old broad and she had her hand broken. After that, she never comes to give me no payments. All the sudden it's this younger one."

Sheen grabbed Grayson's throat and pulled back just enough for an impact when he pushed forward, causing the back of Grayson's head to hit against the bar.

"One more question. Henrietta Childress was murdered. You have anything to do with that?"

Grayson forced the words out, straining through an ever tightening esophagus as he said, "No! I swear!"

Sheen's face turned a violent red as he shouted, "Mickey! The hand!"

Mickey grabbed Grayson's arm and slammed it against the ground, holding it steady. Sheen pulled his Colt from his holster and pointed the barrel point blank at Grayson's hand.

"You wouldn't lie to me, would you, you son of a bitch?" Sheen asked as he shouted in Grayson's face!

"No!" Grayson cried out in fear.

"You don't know anything about that murder?"

"Nothing, I swear! I told you!"

Sheen turned the gun around in his hand and used the butt of the pistol to smash Grayson's hand. The bookie let out a yelp of anguish.

Sheen looked him in the eye and said, "That's for breaking a Lady's hand."

Mickey let go of Grayson's arm as Sheen walked away.

Sheen didn't bother looking back at Grayson as he threatened, "If I find out you're lying to me, we'll be back. Only next time we won't be as friendly."

Mickey unwound his sock and let the billiard balls drop to the floor. One of them caught a portion of Grayson's injured hand as it bounced out. Grayson let out one more whimper.

Mickey smiled as he looked down at Grayson and said, "Nice place you got here. Good location, I think you'll do very well." And then Mickey walked away, leaving Grayson to cradle his wounded hand.

As Sheen and Mickey drove off, they sat in silence. Both exhausted and terribly disappointed that their lead on the bookie proved practically useless.

Mickey reached over and turned on the radio. Sheen lit a Camel as they listened to Bing Crosby and The Andrews Sisters singing "Ac-Cent-Tchu-Ate the Positive".

CHAPTER 9

HENRIETTA CHILDRESS

"**M**r. Childress called," were the words that Mrs. Skeffington greeted Sheen with as he entered the office. "About twenty minutes ago. He asked if you would call back."

"And what did you tell him?" asked Sheen.

"I told him you would."

Sheen's secretary handed him the slip of paper with the message written on it. Sheen took it from her as he raised an eyebrow and said, "Presumptuous."

Mrs. Skeffington huffed and narrowed her stare at him, an angry schoolmarm not taking to the foolish kidding around. Sheen grinned, enjoying the ribbing. He entered his personal office and went directly towards the telephone. Wendell answered the phone and sounded rushed. "Mr. Childress, it's Detective Sheen. Did I catch you at a bad time?" Sheen asked.

"Lunch crowd," Wendell replied. "They keep us hoppin'. I was wonderin' if you had anything new."

"Would it be all right if I came by your shop later?"

"Fine by me."

"Say, about an hour? Things less busy then?"

"Yeah, that's good."

"Fine. See you then."

Sheen hung up the phone and took a seat behind his desk. He made some notes in the file he was keeping in a folder. On the front of the folder, in Mrs. Skeffington's handwriting, were printed the words: Henrietta Childress - June 2, 1952.

A half hour later, Sheen grabbed his fedora, placed it on his head and stepped through the doorway to the outer office. He smiled as he dropped two dollars on Mrs. Skeffington's desk.

"Thanks for the chauffer service this morning. And for putting up with me all the time. Lunch is on me," Sheen said.

Skeffington smiled and said, "I've already had my lunch." She slipped the two dollars in her pocketbook.

"Dinner, then," Sheen said. "Good evening."

⋏ ⋏ ⋏

Sheen arrived at the 7th Street Diner, parked his Coupe out front and went inside. The place was nowhere near as crowded as it had sounded over the phone just an hour ago. Wendell was standing behind the counter, cutting some vegetables. An elderly couple sat at a table near the rear of the restaurant, eating lunch. The young waitress from the first time Sheen had been here served them. She politely smiled at Sheen as she saw him on her way to the kitchen.

"Can I get you a cup of coffee, Detective?" Wendell asked as he wiped tomato juices from his hands.

"That'd be great. Thanks," Sheen said.

As Wendell filled a cup with hot coffee, Sheen mentioned, "I wish I had more news on Henrietta's case for you, but I don't have anything groundbreaking. I have spoken to some people, and eliminated a number of suspects."

Wendell served Sheen the coffee and said, "Well, before you get into it too much, I've asked my sister, Serena, to join us."

"Is that right?" Sheen asked the question, trying to hide his schoolboy excitement while feeling stupid and guilty for having that reaction in the first place.

"So maybe you can wait till she gets here to fill me in."

"No problem." Sheen took a sip of his coffee. "So, do you live around here, Mr. Childress?"

"Got a house over in Richmond Heights," Wendell explained.

Richmond Heights was a private housing development that had been built exclusively for black veterans of the second world war. It had also been commonly known by another nickname...

"The Negro's Shangri-La," Sheen said.

Wendell poured himself a glass of iced water as he responded, "That's what they say."

"You like it over there?"

"When a man's got a home... a place to set up his tired feet, the water comes out the faucet, the lights turn on... he needn't get to complainin', if you take my meaning."

Sheen nodded then asked, "What about Serena? What does she do?"

"Here in the neighborhood, we got a recreational center. Back in the forties, soldiers comin' back from the war, they had a lot of rehabilitation would happen there. Guys who'd lost limbs, learnin' how to do without and carry on. Now we got boys comin' back from Korea needin' the same. Mostly though, she works with neighborhood kids. Lot of them that got fathers overseas and mamas that work. They take the kids out to Virginia Beach and that kind of stuff. She really loves that work, and I believe she's good at it."

"That's swell," Sheen said.

The front door of the diner opened and in walked Serena. She was as fetching in Sheen's eyes as the first time he'd seen her. She showed a pleasant smile to the detective as she saw him sitting at the counter. She approached, a scrapbook in her arms, pressed against her chest, that she laid onto the countertop as she took a seat.

"Hello," she said with a gorgeous smile that Sheen enjoyed seeing. He responded with a hello of his own.

"What do you have for us, Detective?" Wendell asked.

"Well, as I said earlier, not as much as I'd like. I'm afraid the investigation is slow-going. But I was able to speak with a few people and rule out some suspects."

"Oh?"

"Clete Tompkins, the boxer? I have to tell you, I think the kid's clean. He was definitely interested in your sister, but I just don't see him hurting her."

"How can you be sure?" Serena asked.

Sheen turned his attention towards her and plainly stated, "I've been doing this a while and you can generally tell when people have strong feelings and the emotions I detected from Tompkins tell me he was really hung up on your sister. Hurting her is something he could never consider, nor would he want to."

"Okay," Wendell said, "So where does that leave you?"

"Either of you two familiar with The Lady? She was a singer and an acquaintance of your sister."

"Can't say that I am," Wendell responded.

"She didn't really bring us into her professional world," Serena explained. "We were fans of Etta, but *Henrietta* was our sister. She always wanted it that way. She used to say that the people she really loved would know her, but everybody else would see her star."

"I see." Detective Sheen thought to himself that this ideology explained why the names on the list Wendell had provided were mostly friends and family, but not many people outside of their circle of acquaintances.

"Ms. Childress..."

"Please, call me Serena," she insisted.

"That's right, I forgot. Serena, you mentioned last time I was here that this lady..." Sheen pointed to Yunetta Bryce's name on the paper, "She works with you, correct?"

"Yes, Detective."

"Ben, please."

"Okay." Serena smiled pleasantly. Wendell oversaw the interaction and noticed his own discomfort.

Ben continued, "It's my understanding she would go to church with Henrietta?"

"Yes. We would often go together. Wendell and his family too."

"And Ms. Bryce and your sister would then go to Georgette's for Sunday afternoon tea?"

"That's right."

"I'd like to speak with Ms. Bryce."

"Why don't you come around to the recreational hall tomorrow afternoon, she'll be there."

"Terrific. Would you mind writing down the address for me?"

Sheen slid a notepad across the counter and a pen along with it. Serena wrote the address down. Sheen watched her face as she did, but caught himself staring at her eyes, then looked away for fear that Wendell was looking at him. But Wendell hadn't noticed as he was busy pouring a cup of coffee for his sister.

"So what's this about a lady singer?" asked Wendell.

"She's a friend of Henrietta's, thinks the world of her from what I can tell." Sheen thought carefully about how to bring up the darker side of their relationship. "But she's got some problems too. Some health related, others... more questionable. She's a gambler. And it seems that your sister helped her on a number of occasions to pay off some unsavory folks."

Wendell fumed and he looked over at Serena, "You see that! I knew she was in some kind of trouble. That kind of life leads to meetin' the wrong kind of folks."

"Wendell, just settle down," Serena responded.

Wendell turned his attention back towards Sheen and asked, "These people you talkin' about, the ones this lady owed the debt too. They have somethin' to do with Henrietta's murder?"

"Honestly, I don't think so," Sheen flat-out stated. "I spoke with the bookie myself. He had some dealings with Henrietta in the past, on account of The Lady. But he's not in on her death."

"Okay, so where do you go now?"

"I'm going to talk to Ms. Bryce. Then it's going to take some real legwork, since most of what I've found so far really hasn't led me anywhere substantial."

Wendell sighed in frustration. Sheen could not only understand Wendell's irritation, but he shared it to a lesser degree. Sheen didn't like being stuck in the mud on a case any more than a client felt lost when it came to solving the mystery of a loved one's death.

"Mr. Childress," Sheen confided. "I know you're anxious to see this thing through, but I'm working a case that's been cold for three months and I don't have a lot to start with. These things can take a bit of time. You never know when you might lift up the right rock and find what you're looking for. All I can ask is for your patience."

Wendell nodded, still annoyed but what could he do?

Serena moved closer to Sheen, opening the scrapbook she had brought with her. "Ben, I thought you'd like to look through this. Maybe get a better idea who my sister was."

"Sesa, he don't want to be lookin' at that," Wendell abruptly stated. "What's the point?"

"You don't know. Maybe something can help him," Serena insisted.

"I'd like to see it all the same," Sheen replied.

Serena smiled and guided Sheen through the pages of a book filled with pictures as far back as Henrietta's childhood and all the way through her career as Etta Childs. Pictures of Wendell, Henrietta and Serena in their Sunday best for Easter services. One from their childhood, all three standing in front of their house. One picture of Serena and Henrietta, smiling, riding the train on Virginia Beach just a few years ago. When catching a glimpse of that one, Wendell smiled, remembering when he took that photograph.

Much of the rest of the book was pictures and news clippings, lobby cards and movie memorabilia from the career of Etta Childs. Sheen noted that in some of the movie stills and promotional cards, Etta looked different. Serena explained how in the major Hollywood studio films, the producers would make Etta wear heavier powder to appear lighter-skinned on the screen.

Both Serena and Wendell beamed with pride when they got to the page in the book that displayed the lobby card sized poster of the 1949 film *The Homesteaders.* For both Wendell and Serena, this was their favorite of Etta's films. In it she played a woman whose husband has recently passed and the widow fights to keep her farm producing so she can claim the deed to the land outright. The movie took place near the turn of the century and the character had support in her cause from her family, particularly her brother and sister.

It was easy to understand why Serena and Wendell liked the picture so much.

The last image in the book was of the three of them as children, sitting on the front porch. Wendell laying on his stomach, his chin resting on his hands. Serena sat, legs crossed next to him. Henrietta, already growing into her teenage years, stood in a pose, clasping to a towel she had draped over her head. Henrietta was already performing at that age, for her family. The other person in the photograph sat in a rocking chair as she chuckled with delight. This was their mother, Althea.

⊥ ⊥ ⊥

Althea Childress never had it easy. Her husband was lost when her youngest child, Serena, was only five months old. And Althea's other two children were still quite young. Her anger at her husband began when she learned of his criminal activities. Wilton Childress had begun to act erratically. Often paranoid, never sleeping and frequently carrying a pistol hidden beneath his shirt at the waistband of the back of his pants. He had confessed to Althea that his life was in danger. When asked why, he admitted to being a bootlegger and a numbers runner, something he had been for about six years to that point.

Althea was furious with the man and felt more than justified when she smacked him across the face and chest several times in the couples' kitchen. Though no matter how upset and betrayed she felt, his sudden death was not something she wanted. Wilton's enemies had finally caught up with him and disposed of him in a most horrifying manner. The widow Childress dropped to the floor in terror when she opened the package that had been left on her doorstep and contained the severed hands of her husband as well as the extremity representing his manhood.

Althea had always worked. She had been a laundress and seamstress often hired by many of the locals in the much smaller community that was then known as Colored Town. But after her husband's premature death, she sought more consistent employment. That's how Althea found herself taking a job as a chambermaid on Miami Beach. In order to do so, Althea, as all black employees would, had to be issued a card by the Miami Beach Police Department. The card that had her picture and fingerprints on it had to be carried by her at all times while she was working on the beach.

Even before Wilton's murder, Althea was a religious woman. But after the tragedy, her spirituality became an even greater source of comfort and the folks from her congregation were her community and often times the people she could lean on. She sang in the choir at Mt. Zion Baptist church, and years later would often sell food on the avenue with the choir's other members.

One evening, a young Henrietta, just embarking on her teen years, accompanied Althea to the choir's usual spot where they would set up their table. Henrietta helped serve hot fish sandwiches, sweet potato pies and "Sho'nuf" Georgia style barbecue ribs. The folks from Mt. Zion did very well, selling homemade food to folks walking the avenue or yet to get into one of the clubs.

The avenue would jump, lined with people out for their evening's entertainment. Called "The Strip" and "The Great Black Way", 2nd Avenue had a number of places to go and watch the great performers of the day. At the Mary Elizabeth Hotel was The Zebra Lounge. Further on the strip was the Harlem Square Club and over by 7th street was the Cotton Club.

Later in the evening, as sales of food were winding down, Henrietta wandered off and walked around the avenue, amazed by all the sights and sounds. The smell of fish and conch filled the air and the piercing sounds of brass horns carried out each entrance to the clubs that lined the street. Henrietta saw men wooing women who were dressed to the nines, each one looking like a movie star for the evening.

Henrietta passed the alley leading to the rear entrance of the Harlem Square Club when she was distracted by the impromptu performance of three musicians who had stepped outside the club. They were showing each other some improvised riffs, one on a trumpet, the others with saxophones. They laughed and joked with each other between exploring musical phrases, three jazz men constantly dedicated to the joy of their art.

Henrietta stepped further down the alley to get a closer look. She smiled in wonder as she watched the trio.

"Mama's sugar the sweetest you ever tasted. But nobody gets it lest they know how to treat The Lady," a voice stated at the rear entrance to the club. Henrietta turned her head and saw a beautiful, statuesque woman in her late thirties with sensual eyes and an inescapable glow about her. She wore a stunning silver sequined dress and had a string of pearls draped around her neck. In her perfectly coifed hair, she had a yellow rose, which stuck out ever so slightly. The woman, a performer named Marguerite Sloane, saw young Henrietta standing in the alley. She smiled at the nearly teen-aged girl and asked, "What's your name, darling?"

"Henrietta," the girl replied.

"Well, Henrietta. You are something beautiful."

"Thank you, ma'am."

"What you doing out here by yourself, honey?"

"I ain't. I'm with my Mama. She's selling food with the church group on the avenue."

"Is that right? Well you best get on back to her before she starts to worrying."

"Yes, ma'am."

Marguerite stepped closer to Henrietta and pulled the yellow rose out of her hair. She kneeled down and gently placed the rose over Henrietta's ear as she said, "You are the sweetest thing. And now you are the prettiest woman on the avenue and don't let nobody tell you different, because The Lady says so."

Henrietta smiled and even blushed a little. Marguerite held Henrietta's chin between her thumb and her forefinger. The performer looked into the child's eyes and said, "Girls like us, we got to let our star shine as bright as we want it to." Marguerite kissed Henrietta on the forehead. "Now run along."

"Thank you," Henrietta replied. She walked away. Neither lady could have known at that moment that years later Henrietta would be the one to help Marguerite after she'd fallen on hard times. Henrietta never forgot the encounter, but wouldn't mention to The Lady that they'd once met on the avenue. Henrietta assumed The Lady wouldn't remember it and rather liked not knowing that for a fact.

That evening when Henrietta returned to the empty lot where the Mt. Zion choir had set up their table, her mother raised her voice when she asked, "Henrietta Mae, where have you been?"

Henrietta was all smiles as she showed Althea the rose and said, "Look what this lady gave me! She told me..."

Whack! Henrietta was interrupted by the force of Althea's tough hands slapping her across the face. "Don't you never go runnin' off like that again! You had me worried sick!"

Henrietta felt the shame of being disobedient, immediately deflating the joy of her encounter. Lowering her head, with a long face, she responded, "Yes, Mama."

⅄ ⅄ ⅄

Throughout her teen years, Henrietta would continue to be fascinated by the lives of performers. She loved the picture shows and tried to go as often as she could sneak away. And she sang, constantly. Everywhere she went a melody would escape her lips. By the time she was of age she competed for the honor of Coconut Queen. The activities surrounding the Orange Bowl in Miami each year were mostly closed to black people and so the community held the Coconut Festival. The events included an all-black football game at Dorsey Park on 1st avenue and a parade led by the Coconut Queen down 2nd avenue. Henrietta won quite a few admirers, looking as beautiful as she did during her evening as Queen.

By the time Serena was at the age of twelve, she had noticed the differences in her older sister. Henrietta had developed and men around her noticed as well. One Saturday afternoon she followed Henrietta and a young man as they walked away from a picnic gathering of Althea's co-workers. Serena saw Henrietta and the awe-struck admirer step between the trees that bordered a large wooded area. Though curious, Serena decided to return to the gathering. But after a time, Althea asked where Henrietta had gone and sent Serena to fetch her.

Serena quietly stepped into the brush covered terrain and walked past a few trees. She heard the sounds of kisses and whimpers. She followed the noises and peeked behind a recently sprouted palm tree. Her sister lay on the ground beneath the young man whose bare ass was being clenched by Henrietta's long legs wrapped around him. The dark nipple on Henrietta's right breast was pushed out over her brassiere and stood erect as her lover flicked it with his wet tongue. Serena was smart enough to know that this must be sex. She was embarrassed to watch, but unable to look away. There was a tightness in her stomach. The same combination of excitement and shame that she felt when she herself would use her hand to fondle her privates in the bath tub.

"Girls? Where are you?" Althea shouted.

Serena ducked down to the ground and turned to look the other way. Henrietta and her lover were startled by the call and Henrietta shoved him off of her, getting up on her knees, while fully dressing.

Serena called out, "Henrietta! Mama wants you!"

A look of surprise crept across Henrietta's face. "Okay. I'll be right there."

"Come on, baby. I'm almost done," begged the infatuated young man.

Serena looked over her shoulder and peeked through the palm fronds to see Henrietta smile at him. Her smile was seductive and her eyes commanding. Henrietta reached down and grabbed his erect penis, massaging it back and forth. She leaned in and with her lips pressed against his cheek she said, "Come on. Do it for me, daddy."

The man reached his climax, his eyes rolling back in his head as he grunted a few powerful breaths. Henrietta smiled at what she had done.

Serena didn't actually pay much attention to the fact that this was the first time she'd seen male genitalia, let alone the orgasmic conclusion that happens when it's aroused. Rather she was focused on her older sister. She recognized something in that look on her face. It was the fact that Henrietta adored being adored. Knowing that being who she was could wrap people around her finger was something Henrietta enjoyed.

Serena ran out of the woods, towards the picnic area. Henrietta followed moments later.

⅄ ⅄ ⅄

Henrietta's fondness for the admiration of others continued when she started working at the Monarch Diner. Her customers were often pleased just to sit and watch her take their lunch and dinner orders and hear her lovely voice as she sang moving to and from the kitchen. Of course it wasn't just that she was such a beauty, but she had a sweet disposition and always had time to speak to anyone who came in and had something to talk about. Clifford Dee was pleased and proud to have Henrietta working for him. And he was the first to predict that she would be a star someplace. He just figured it would be on the Avenue, singing in the clubs.

One evening, when Henrietta was twenty years old, the talk around the diner was about a young black man from a few counties north of Miami that had been lynched for failing to refer to a white man as "Mr." The young man was shot and thrown in a river. He had been home visiting his parents during a semester break from Morehouse College.

Henrietta was disturbed by the news, but further hated seeing how much it affected the diner patrons and its owner Mr. Dee. She didn't like seeing people upset. Especially when, despite her best efforts, she couldn't cheer them up.

That night after Henrietta had returned home from her job waiting tables at the diner and her Mother had come from Miami Beach where she cleaned hotel bedrooms and restrooms, they talked about the upsetting news that was on everyone in the black community's minds.

Serena and Wendell listened to the discussion, neither having as advanced an opinion as the older Childresses. Wendell was just barely sixteen and Serena a couple years younger. Serena was well aware of the dangers of discrimination and the segregated society in which she lived, but still had some naiveté about the harsh realities of the adult world. Wendell was just angry, recognizing that the laws of the land were unjust towards him and felt an unspoken bond with the victim of the lynching, being a young black man.

Henrietta shook her head and said, "Everybody I know, that's all they got to speak on today. Terrible thing, isn't it, Mama?"

Althea sat back in her chair, resting a weary body. Her leg was propped up, laid across the knee of the other one as she rubbed the bottom of her heel. She simply nodded in agreement with her oldest child.

Henrietta continued, "All the folks in the diner today... the whole place was filled up with nothing but sadness. It's never like that."

Serena quietly spoke up, "What about that boy's mama and daddy? They got to be devastated."

Wendell looked over at his younger sister, impressed but curious and asked, "Where'd you learn that word?"

Serena shrugged. "I read it in a book from the library."

Althea smiled as she looked at Serena. Henrietta continued the conversation, "I'm sure those folks are grieving something awful."

Althea replied, "Baby, folks like us is born grieving. Our peoples been slaves, been lynched, been made to live with less 'cause we black. But nary is a day gone by that our spirits ain't lifted. 'Cause we talk to God and he listens to all his children."

Henrietta thought on that as she stared at her mother. Althea leaned her head on the top of the chair's back and closed her eyes for a moment. She lowered her leg and started to lift the other one up.

"Mama," Serena said. "Do you want me to do the other one for you?"

Althea smiled and responded, "If you don't mind, baby."

Serena sat on the ground in front of her mother's chair and proceeded to rub her feet. Henrietta saw how tired her mother was, knowing how hard she worked. And now Henrietta had become a hard worker as well. But she knew she wanted to do other things with her life and felt she had kept it to herself for too long.

"Mama," Henrietta nervously said. "I want more than this. I don't mean to sound like I don't appreciate everything you've done and what we got. But I want better for myself in life. And for all of us."

Althea dismissed it with a wave of her hand. "Henrietta you're too old to send to college. If we lucky we can get both your brother and sister to go, but that's all there is to it."

"That's not what I mean. Mama, I want to be in the pictures. Be on the stage."

Althea sighed. Dreams had no place in this world and her daughter was too old for them anyhow. "Henrietta, nobody comes from around here that gets to be a movie star."

Henrietta stood up, walked across the room and reached into a dresser drawer. "That's not true," she insisted. She pulled a magazine out of the drawer and turned to a page. "There's this new actress in a movie with Ray Milland and the actor from *Golden Boy*." Henrietta handed the magazine to her mother.

"She went to Miami High School," Henrietta pointed out.

Althea looked at the page in the magazine. It was an advertisement for a new Paramount Pictures release titled *I Wanted Wings*. The sultry actress in the advertisement, with her blond hair hanging halfway over her face was a newcomer named Veronica Lake.

Althea handed the magazine back to Henrietta and said, "She is beautiful."

"So am I, Mama."

"Not to white folk, baby. And if'n you is, you gonna be one of them acceptable Negro types. Not no damn movie star!"

"You're wrong. My star can shine as bright as I want it to. Hollywood, things aren't like they are here. Hattie McDaniel just won the academy award!"

"Mm-hmm. Playin' a slave. A smiley-faced house nigger."

Henrietta's heart sank. She wanted her mother to see the endless possibilities that she envisioned for herself, but Althea couldn't imagine them. It wasn't Althea's way of being mean, she merely wanted to protect her child from disappointment. Henrietta's aspirations were too foreign to the world that Althea knew.

But Henrietta felt a bitterness towards her mother, misinterpreting her motives. Henrietta thought her mother was trying to keep her from flourishing. She believed Althea wanted to keep her in their small town, in the community. She even wondered if Althea's church-going ways had something to do with keeping Henrietta away from Hollywood. Either way, Henrietta always resented the fact that she never felt support from Althea.

Though Althea lived long enough to see Henrietta become a popular local performer at the clubs on the avenue, she died of heart failure a few years before Henrietta made her debut in the pictures. When she passed on, Henrietta was in St. Louis performing on a road tour with a local jazz quintet. Wendell was overseas and Althea died not knowing if her son would ever come home from the war in Europe. Only Serena, who had taken care of her in her final months, was by her side.

🙼 🙼 🙼

The last time Serena had seen Henrietta before her murder was at New Year's. As 1951 became 1952, the sisters were enjoying an evening of music at the Rockland Palace where Snookum Russell led the house band. In a rare moment of candidness, Serena admitted to Henrietta that she had seen her with that young man at the picnic all those years ago. Henrietta was embarrassed to hear it but said she had wondered about that.

This led to Henrietta asking about Serena's love life. Serena tried to dodge the question but Henrietta said, "I worry about you. You're so beautiful and you have such a great heart. You were always the best of all of us and you should share that with some lucky man."

Serena smiled. Henrietta continued, "Fall in love, sister. Believe me. Nothing else in this life is worth anything once you know what love really is."

Serena gave her sister a look that accentuated her question, "You telling me you in love with someone?"

The smile that crossed Henrietta's face was one Serena had never seen before. The other men that Henrietta had been with had always brought out the personal pleasure she felt in being adored. But this was the look of someone who adored another and was constantly happy about it.

Henrietta put the focus back on her sister and said, "Honey, I just want you to be happy. You deserve that."

Henrietta reached across the table and pulled her sister forward for a hug. Serena smiled. Henrietta was about to release the embrace, but Serena wouldn't let her go. For some reason Serena felt this hug meant everything to her, though she didn't understand why.

"I love you," Serena said.

Henrietta found the moment odd, but touching. She kissed her baby sister on the check and said, "I love you, too."

A month later, Serena would be sitting in Henrietta's house in Brownsville, waiting with her sister's body for the funeral home to send a car.

CHAPTER 10

Truths and Taboos

Detective Sheen pulled his Coupe up to the curb outside the recreational center around midday. He stepped out of his car, but not until he had thoroughly checked his appearance and made sure his hair was neatly combed.

He entered the building and looked around, seeing a number of disabled veterans. Some were involved in conversation with each other, a few drank coffee as they read through the daily news. A small group stood near a ping-pong table, either playing or awaiting their turns.

An older black gentleman approached, gray hair starting to fill around his temples and eyeglasses balanced on the bridge of his nose. He asked Sheen, "Sir? Something you need here?"

Sheen smiled and replied, "Yes. I'm looking for Seren…" Sheen censored himself, fearing the informality might be misunderstood. "Ms. Childress. I was asked to come and speak to her this afternoon."

"Follow me," the man said, as he led Sheen through a pair of double doors and down a long hallway lined with rooms on one side and windows showing the modest patch of lawn outside, with a few trees that had grown up in the area.

At the end of the corridor, the man opened a door and pointed towards a table at the front of a room filled with children. "Right over there," the man instructed.

"Thank you, very much," the detective said as he nodded his head at the fellow. He approached the table and Serena looked up, seeing him walk over. She smiled, a gesture Sheen found to be quite pleasant. His instincts told him that she was happy to see him.

"Good afternoon," he said as he stood by her table.

Serena stood up and responded, "Hello Detective. Pardon me... Ben." Sheen returned her smile.

"You've come to see Ms. Bryce, is that right?"

"Yes."

"Let's go see if she has a few minutes to spare."

Serena walked away and Sheen followed close behind. As they crossed the room, the detective's eye was caught by a board game that four of the children were playing.

"That seems like a clever game," he commented. Serena stopped and looked at the boys' game. The board was homemade, carved from a piece of plywood. A line of circular indentations formed the outline of a cross that covered much of the board. An additional circle sat in the center of the board and four circles were located diagonally at each corner. At the center of each end of the "t" were four more holes. The boys played the game with marbles and each time one rolled a six-sided die, he would move the marble the corresponding amount of spaces on the board.

"Mm-hmm. A lady that used to work here brought it back with her one summer after visiting her people up around Altoona. Some sort of Appalachian game, but the kids all seem to love it."

Serena and Sheen continued on. Ben looked back over his shoulder when he heard one of the boys roll the die and exclaim, "I kill you! Back to your home!" One of the other boys removed his marble from the middle of the board and placed it in one of the diagonal rows.

Yunetta Bryce sat at a modest desk with a variety of forms stacked on top of it. She was approaching forty but worked very hard to look ten years younger, nearly achieving that goal.

Serena said, "Yunetta. This is the detective I told you about, Mr. Sheen. He's looking into Henrietta's murder."

Yunetta extended her hand and Sheen shook it. "Ma'am," he said. "It's nice to meet you."

"You too, Detective," Yunetta responded. "Please, have a seat."

"Thank you." Sheen sat across the desk from her.

"Well," Serena interjected. "I'll just leave you to it."

Sheen smiled at Serena as he thanked her for the introduction. Serena smiled back, lingered for a moment, then walked away. Sheen kept his gaze on her for a few seconds before turning his attention back to Ms. Bryce.

"So, how does this work? It's a first for me," Yunetta said.

"Just a few questions, Ms. Bryce," Sheen responded.

The detective held his notepad in front of him and referred to it as he asked, "Did Henrietta Childress talk to you much about her personal life?"

"Yes," her responses were hesitant at first. "Sometimes."

"You frequented at Georgette's Tea Room with her, typically on Sunday afternoons. Is that correct?"

"Yes."

"Anybody else that you ladies socialized with there?"

"We had some folks we'd talk to. But never any serious personal matters. More friendly like, you know? Things about town, in the community. Music and movies, that sort of thing."

"So you wouldn't say that there was anyone else that Henrietta confided in?"

"Not that I know of. She talked to me quite a bit. And, of course, Serena. And then there's The Lady."

"Yes, I've already spoken with her. Ms. Bryce, in all your discussions with Ms. Childress, did she talk at all about her romantic life?"

Yunetta Bryce was not one to gossip. She anticipated that this question was coming and she lowered her head to stare down her nose at Sheen. She studied him and carefully thought about her response. "Detective, I am not in the habit of discussing the delicate matters of others."

"I understand, ma'am."

"I want you to know this, because it is very hard for me to talk about other people and things that, frankly, are usually nobody else's business. So I have to ask you... Do you honestly believe this information will help you solve Henrietta's murder?"

Sheen looked Ms. Bryce in the eye and as directly as possible told her, "Yes. I do."

Yunetta sighed, nodded her head ever so slightly, then continued, "Very well. What would you like to know?"

"Well, I've looked into this young man, Clete Tompkins. He's a boxer, had a crush on Ms. Childress..."

"Yes, I know all about Clete."

"What did Henrietta think of him?"

"She thought he was sweet. She liked to talk with him, liked the way he listened to her. I think she could have had an interest in Clete if she wasn't already... well..."

"She was in love, wasn't she?"

"Yes. Very much so."

"Is his name Nate?"

"Yes."

"Do you know him?"

"No. Henrietta never introduced me. But she spoke of him very often. She needed someone to talk to and... I don't know, I guess she felt safe talking with me."

"Safe? Talking about her gentleman friend? Why wouldn't she feel safe speaking with others about him?"

Yunetta was troubled, conflicted in her expression as she stared at Sheen, but had to put faith in his investigation and proceeded. "This is not the easiest thing for some to hear. And I don't know how Serena or her brother will take it. Honestly, I don't know how you will... But Nate is, well he's like you, Mr. Sheen."

Sheen asked, "He's a detective? Or police?"

Yunetta shook her head and corrected the misunderstanding, "No. He's white."

⋏ ⋏ ⋏

Later, after Sheen had thanked Yunetta Bryce for her help, he found himself standing near his car, at the front of the building with Serena.

"So was Ms. Bryce able to help you?" Serena asked.

"Yes, I believe she was," Sheen replied.

"My sister was adored by many, but only a few people knew her very well. I mean, really knew who she was."

"Yes. Ms. Bryce indicated that you were one of those people."

Serena shrugged. "On some things, yes. But not always. I'd never heard of The Lady 'til you told me and Wendell about her. And I didn't know about Clete Tompkins."

"And you've said you didn't know Nate."

"That's right. See, I guess there's plenty about my sister that I didn't know."

"Did you know if she was in love with someone before her passing?"

Serena thought on it and remembered that last conversation at New Year's. "Henrietta seemed like she wanted to tell me that she was in love with someone. But, for some reason, she didn't go into it very much. I wondered about that, especially after her murder. One of those conversations you regret never having until it's too late... I never understood why she didn't talk to me about it."

Sheen wasn't sure of his footing here. Was it his place to reveal this secret about Henrietta's lover? Outside of the potential bearing it had on the case, what was the importance of it? And who was he to relay this news to Henrietta's grieving sister? If Henrietta hadn't told Serena and Wendell, she'd obviously had her reasons. Was it just fear that their reaction would be devastating to her, or did she have other reasons not to mention it?

Serena extended her hand and said, "Thank you for the work you are doing on the case, Ben. Just knowing that the police investigation is not the only one out there... I don't know, it comforts me to see someone trying to get to the bottom of her murder."

Sheen accepted her hand and shook it. "It's what I do. And I'll try everything I can think of until it's solved." Sheen didn't let go of Serena's hand. He didn't want to. He stared at her eyes, noticing that she was staring back. He didn't have time to find the courage to ask, as his desire overwhelmed any doubt or sense of logic on the matter. He blurted out, "Would you like to get some dinner?"

After he heard himself utter the words, he immediately felt the discomfort for having asked. Not sure if it was completely inappropriate to do so. He'd worried he offended Serena, as a white man asking her to dinner. His fears were soothed when she smiled at him and said, "Yes."

Fifteen minutes later Sheen held the front door of The Patriot Diner open for Serena. She smiled and thanked him for the courtesy.

Sheen motioned with his index and forefinger, forming a 'v' as he said to the hostess, "Table for two, please."

The hostess, nervous and not hiding it well, turned her attention to the man behind the counter. A sea of upturned white faces stared at the ethnically diverse duo at the front door in wonder and amazement. The man behind the counter, a stern look on his face shook his head. He waved his index finger back and forth and said, "You can stay. But we won't serve the colored. She'll have to wait outside."

Sheen's ancestral ruddy complexion deepened. He rotated his shoulders back, causing them to crack and he scowled at the proprietor as he said, "Is that so?"

Serena placed her hand on his arm, nudging him back. She said, "It's fine. We'll go someplace else. I know someplace better."

Sheen held his stare on the man. Serena urged him back again. Sheen opened the door for Serena and let her walk out before him, but he never took his eyes off the man at the counter.

⌄ ⌄ ⌄

Friendly's Barbecue Stand was located just a few blocks northwest of Sheen's office. On NW 8th street it fringed on the area where Overtown became Downtown Miami, nearly neutral between black and white communities. It was named Friendly's in the 1920s, back when it was just a couple of picnic tables, outdoor style, with a big barbecue pit off to the side. The man who ran the place was named Delmond Friendly. He'd long since passed, but the man who now ran it also went by the name Friendly, for good business. And it was no longer a traditional stand. Now it was an actual restaurant structure with indoor dining and outdoor tables, screened in to keep the mosquitoes away. But the food was just as good as it ever was.

"Ms. Childress," said a lovely older black woman for whom maternal instinct was practically a physical description. Her name was

Deana Laroux, and she was the wife of the current owner, the new "Mr. Friendly", Albert.

Deana, who was as kind as could be, hugged Serena. "Sweet thing, it's been too long since you been up in here."

Serena smiled and said, "It's nice to see you, Miss Laroux".

Deana dropped her arms from around Serena to grab both her hands. She affectionately squeezed them as she told Serena, "We was so sorry to hear about your sister. Henrietta was such a darling woman. The world ain't as right without her."

"Thank you."

Deana looked at the man alongside Serena, had a moment's pause, wherein she batted an eye at Serena, then politely asked, "And who is this gentleman?"

"This is Detective Sheen. He's working on the case of Henrietta's murder," Serena replied. Then introduced, "This is Deana Laroux. Her and her husband own this place."

"Well, true as that is we won't talk about it. I like to let Mr. Friendly think he's in charge of everything."

The trio laughed and Sheen extended his hand. "Pleasure to meet you, ma'am."

Deana shook his hand and said, "I hope y'all is hungry."

"Yes, indeed," Sheen admitted.

Deana led them to a table where they sat and placed their order. Serena had the barbecue chicken with okra and tomatoes and a glass of sweet tea, while Sheen ordered the ribs with macaroni & cheese and red beans & rice, washed down with a glass of homemade lemonade. And both shared a basket of corn bread muffins.

"It seems like you and your brother are pretty close," Sheen observed.

"Yes," Serena replied. "It's always been that way with my family. What about you? You have any people around?"

Sheen shrugged and explained, "Nobody in these parts. Got a brother in Chicago, works in the stock market. Parents are long gone... I had a wife for a time, and a son."

Serena was surprised to hear this and was curious to know more, but didn't want to impose by asking. Instead, she looked at him and let him take the conversation in whatever direction he chose to.

Sheen continued, "Not long after I got back from the war, she was with child. I was working for the police department at the time. We bought our house and things seemed to be going well. He was barely three years old when he got sick and eventually passed on. For a time my wife tried to get through it, but she was drifting further away. Finally she turned to drugs to cope. And her addiction only got worse with time. I did all I could to try helping her, but nothing would work. Our marriage wasn't much of a relationship after Matthew died. She didn't want my help, or at least she didn't take it. One day I came home and she was gone. That was a little over two years ago and I haven't seen her since."

"My goodness. I had no idea. I don't know what to say."

Sheen half-smiled at her and offered, "Isn't much to say about it. I've come to terms as much as I can. We aren't supposed to outlive our children, that's not the way of things. But sometimes it's reality. And Opal couldn't cope with that. I used to wonder if she would just show up out of nowhere someday. But I don't give it much thought anymore. It had gotten bad between us and I've come to realize that it was probably better off that she left."

"Matthew's a lovely name."

Sheen nodded. "Him I miss every day. There's no getting around that."

The duo enjoyed conversation and took time with their meal, staying at the restaurant for well over two hours. They found that they'd liked some of the same music, particularly Cab Calloway and the harmonic sounds of The Mills Brothers. And they were both fans of the old Charlie Chaplin films, though they had agreed they'd missed his Little Tramp character and neither of them particularly liked his last picture, *Monsieur Verdoux,* from a few years back. However both were curious to see his latest movie, *Limelight.*

Mr. Friendly had walked over to the table to say hello to Serena. He expressed his sympathy for Henrietta's passing and Serena thanked him before introducing Ben as the detective investigating her murder.

Friendly and Sheen shook hands and the detective said, "Mr. Friendly, this is by far the best barbecue I have ever tasted."

"Thank you, sir," Mr. Friendly responded. "We work hard to keep our customers happy. But y'all ought to do yourselves a favor and try Mrs. Laroux's blueberry pie."

Sheen and Serena obliged and enjoyed the homemade slices of pie with two cups of coffee. As they left the restaurant and walked towards Sheen's car, he said, "It's been wonderful speaking with you. I enjoyed myself very much."

"It was a very lovely evening," Serena said. Sheen opened the passenger door for her. She thanked him and smiled that same smile that quickened his breath each time he saw it. Without thinking about who he was, who she was and where they were, Sheen placed a hand on her waist, leaned in and kissed her on the lips. Moments after he noticed that she was kissing him back, he remembered the world around them and pulled back, looking around the area with absolutely no subtlety.

Serena stared at him then offered, "Do you have anything to drink at your place?"

Sheen locked eyes with her and gently nodded. Serena got in the car and Sheen briskly walked around to the driver's side. He got in, started the car and drove off.

⅄ ⅄ ⅄

Sheen led Serena into his house. She was immediately introduced to Doyle, who had jogged towards the door the moment they had entered. Doyle liked her immediately, wagging his tail and rubbing his head against the side of her leg. She petted him and Sheen patted his back saying, "All right, Doyle. That's enough, boy."

Doyle sauntered back towards the kitchen and laid down on the floor.

Sheen moved towards the kitchen and said, "I know I have whiskey, but... perhaps there is some brandy in the..."

"Whiskey is fine," Serena said before he had to make the effort to find another option. Sheen nodded and said, "Coming right up. I have some music if you'd like to put something on, right over there."

Sheen pointed to the RCA Victor Victrola that he had purchased in 1946. In its advertisements, it stated that it had the "Golden Throat", new RCA Victor FM radio reception and the exclusive "Silent Sapphire" pickup.

As Sheen placed ice cubes in two glasses and poured their cocktails from the bottle that was labeled "Jameson Irish Whiskey", Serena inspected the collection of records at the phonograph cabinet. She selected a 45 with the burgundy colored Commodore label, with its white and gold printing listing the single as "How am I to Know?", a 1944 recording by Billie Holiday.

She placed the record on the turntable, placed the needle on the outer edge of the disc and closed her eyes as the majestic flick of a few high-pitched piano notes was followed by a collection of horns.

Sheen stepped forward, two glasses of whiskey in his hands and said, "That's a wonderful song." Serena opened her eyes and replied, "Yes."

He handed her a glass and she took a sip. Sheen watched her place her lips to the rim of the glass and noticed the smudge of her lipstick that remained after she finished her sip.

Both were nervous, both about to experience something new and both were excited to do so. Serena was not a very experienced woman when it came to making love, but was certainly not totally innocent about it either. She hadn't been a virgin since 1941 when her then boyfriend Amos Huxley was about to ship off to the war and tried to convince her that he might not make it back, and they may never have the chance to make love again. Serena didn't sleep with him because of his attempt to leverage his military service into sexual sympathy. In fact, she had been ready to try sex for quite some time, but felt guilty about giving in easily to any man who wanted it. Amos Huxley had just given her the excuse to lose her virginity with as little self inflicted guilt as possible.

But all of her experiences had been with black men, and her curiosity was certainly part of her attraction. She had never seen a white penis before, and wondered what it might look like. And she was not alone in the questions running through her mind. Sheen was equally curious about her. Sheen wondered if the feeling and the taste of Serena's skin would be different. And being a man who enjoyed going down on women, he wondered about that taste as well.

His predilection for that act was something he had done without during his marriage, as his wife did not like it. She felt it was too raunchy, almost uncivilized. Sheen did feel his wife had been a very uptight lover. He recalled that the most immense erection he ever had was when a woman he was orally pleasing in France during the war had several orgasms.

Sheen took a sip of his whiskey as Serena walked closer to him and placed her hand flat against his chest. It was near his heart and she could feel the rapidity of its beating. Sheen put his glass down on the table and took Serena's glass as well. He held his hand on top of hers and with the other he touched her cheek. They began to kiss, slowly and with a gentle sweetness meant to savor the moment. Their kisses became more passionate and within a few moments, Serena's hands were clasped around the sides of Sheen's face and he had his arms wrapped around her waist. He pulled her closer to him and they moved in the direction of the bedroom. She raised her legs and Sheen held her up beneath her thighs, the two of them collapsing into the soft mattress that lay on Sheen's bed frame.

They slowed down in pace as they both undressed, taking in all the sights of a new nakedness they had never before experienced. A sly smile crept across Serena's face as she saw the half stiffened white penis between Sheen's legs, with its pinkish, purple tip, the remainder of its erection being fulfilled as Sheen gazed upon the dark brown nipples on the end of Serena's full breasts.

Sheen kissed her neck, then her chest, her breasts and the front and sides of her stomach. He moved further down to her lap and her thighs, before opening her legs and kissing her pussy. He was fascinated by the tiny buds of curls that covered her pubis, kinky and black. He was pleased to learn that she did taste different, as he had wondered she might. In fact he thought she tasted better, the sweetest he'd ever had.

After he had satisfied her with his tongue, she grabbed his penis, stroking it. She rubbed the swollen tip up against her clitoris, feeling it become more erect in her grasp. She inserted his cock and he continually pushed it inside her until it pulsated to an orgasmic release.

They laid together for another twenty minutes, not speaking, but holding each other. Cuddled up in a spoon position, Sheen would occasionally kiss the back of her neck and her shoulders. He licked the trail of sweat that had trickled down her spine. This excited him further and Serena could feel his erection starting to grow against her body. She wiggled her hips ever so slightly, rubbing his hard penis against her full, round buttocks. Sheen reached around between Serena's thighs and put two fingers inside her, feeling her wetness.

They made love twice more before falling asleep in each other's arms.

CHAPTER 11

WHAT THE G-MEN KNEW

Sheen woke from what seemed like the best sleep he'd had in months, maybe years. He casually walked into the bathroom and splashed some cold water on his face. When he stepped into the kitchen, he saw Doyle sitting on the floor, a pitiful stare up at the beautiful woman at the counter. Doyle looked back at his master with a plea of help. "I'm not sure he likes me very much," Serena said. "I put some food out for him and he hasn't eaten."

Doyle looked at the dog bowl and the canned food that had been slopped into it. Then, his pitiful expression made its way back towards Sheen.

"He, uh... he has a very different diet from most."

"I see," replied Serena. Then there was a knock at the front door.

"Excuse me, won't you?" Sheen headed to the house's entrance and opened the door. Standing outside on the porch, waiting for a response was Sheen's former partner, Detective Tierney. Instincts kicked in for Sheen as he nonchalantly pulled the door closed behind him and stepped out on the porch.

"Hey, partner. What brings you around?" Sheen asked.

"Old friends. I don't know, I felt sort of bad when you asked for my help and I had to railroad you a bit."

"I'm not sore at you, if that's what you're thinking."

"I didn't think you were, but nonetheless, I wanted to help you. Trouble is the department's got more eyes and ears to dodge than when you were there. Can't be too careful when it comes to orders. You know what a son of a bitch Granville is. And he's got friends with big pants."

"So you've got something you can tell me outside the office, that it?"

"Yeah. Your Negro actress that got herself killed. She's got some interesting acquaintances. The kind that the hot dogs at the Bureau like to look into."

"She into something illegal?"

"That depends on whose standards you're looking at and whether you still believe in the burden of proof. Now I don't know much, on account that I never could get a look at the file. But the girl was a friend of Robeson's. Voiced her support of his talents, though never gave any political statements. One social point she agreed with was Robeson's opinions on how Negros are treated in America, and had stood by his passionate pursuing of anti-lynching legislation. It's no secret that Robeson's considered a menace by Hoover's guys and apparently the eyes on him extend to those anywhere near him. Just thought you should know."

The actor Paul Robeson had been considered to be un-American, after his associations with a number of political and social movements that were listed by the attorney general as subversive to the American way of being. Sheen could imagine how any connection to him could be detrimental to a rising star like Etta. It was also no surprise to him that J. Edgar Hoover might be investigating an actress who lived part-time in Miami. After all, Mr. Hoover himself had once referred to Miami as "a Mecca for hoodlums." Hoover's opinion of the Magic City was not a high one.

The best-known secret throughout the many stages of law enforcement was how the FBI agents, as per Hoover's instruction, strenuously investigated any and all perceived threats to American democracy and morality. This included a number of actors and writers. And with Senator Joseph McCarthy of Wisconsin leading a nationally glorified hunt for communist threats, Hoover's investigations fit right in with the nation's mood.

After Sheen thanked Tierney for the tip, he went inside to place a call to an old friend. During the war he'd struck up a friendship that would become the life-long variety that no amount of time apart would ever alter. Richard Levesque had joined the 82nd airborne division shortly after Sheen. During combat in the Battle of the Bulge, a fallen tree in the Ardennes Forest that had been knocked down as a result of intense shelling, became an obstruction for Richard. He had somehow managed to get his foot wedged between the trunk and the snow-covered ground. Richard later remembered having lost his footing while running for cover from artillery fire. Snow shifted beneath his boots and the tree must have rolled ever so slightly, but enough to trap him in place. Sheen looked back and called after Richard. He could see that his fellow soldier was stuck and retreated to help dislodge Richard's foot.

As soon as he was free, Richard joined Sheen in running for protection from the German offense. Less than a minute after they'd cleared away from the area, a shell landed a half of a foot away from the downed tree and exploded the grounds around it. Richard immediately felt indebted to Sheen for saving his life and told Ben that if he ever needed anything at all, to never hesitate to ask. A sentiment that could be helpful, now that Levesque was an agent with the Bureau of Investigation.

Sheen wasn't entirely comfortable using the "I saved your life, can you let me look at one of the bureau's files" approach, but he felt the missing pieces of information that he needed could very well be in that file. Sheen tried to be as coy as possible, and Richard was a sharp guy so he knew what Sheen wanted him to do. Richard simply said, "Give me a name." And Sheen gave the name of Henrietta Childress and added that she was a Negro actress with the stage name of Etta Childs.

"Okay, Ben." Richard's voice instructed over the phone, "I'll be in on the train tomorrow, late morning. Let's get together for lunch, and then I'll see what I can do for you. Take down this address."

"Sure, pal. Just a second," Sheen said as he turned towards Serena. He made a gesture with his hand to signify that he needed a pencil. Then he pointed to an old-fashioned dining room cupboard, which had two drawers beneath the displayed plates. Serena opened one of the drawers, in search of a pencil, but instead finding a framed picture of a young boy playing in a yard. Sheen snapped his fingers and pointed to the other drawer. Serena opened that one and found a pencil, which she quickly handed to Sheen.

Richard gave Sheen the address to a place called The Trio Diner, on southwest 8th street and 36th court. It was a restaurant that Agent Levesque had frequented while on assignment in Miami, investigating organized crime. Sheen was to meet Richard there the next day at 11:30 AM.

After Sheen hung up, Serena re-opened the first drawer and held up the picture of the little boy. She asked, "Is this your son?"

Sheen looked at the picture and gave a gentle nod. "That's Matthew."

Serena looked at the picture and smiled, "He seems like a sweet child."

"He was."

"What did he like to do? His interests?"

"He didn't live long enough to develop any... preferences." Sheen thought for a moment, remembering and immediately correcting himself when saying, "He liked to draw. He was always drawing pictures, every chance he got."

"Why do you keep this picture hidden in the drawer?"

Sheen stared at Serena, almost embarrassed to say, "Memories are painful."

"Some pain is the kind we need," she responded. She took another look at the picture then replaced it in the drawer and shut it. "Could you give me a ride to the recreation center? We're taking the boys to a charity game at Miami Stadium."

"Is that so?"

"Yes." Serena saw the curiosity in Sheen's eyes and asked, "Would you like to go?"

人 人 人

At the recreation center, Serena introduced Ben as Mr. Sheen to the group of a dozen young black boys. She left them to get acquainted as she went over the last minute preparations with the bus driver. Sheen talked to the boys and asked them how they liked spending time at the center. The boys mostly seemed excited about being there and talked about enjoying the games they played and some of the arts and crafts they worked on. Several of the boys had their baseball gloves ready to take with them for the afternoon's outing. A few tossed the ball around and one exclaimed, "I'm gonna be a baseball player! I'm gonna play for the Brooklyn Dodgers, just like Jackie Robinson!" The other boys cheered, insisting they were going to do the same.

"Oh yeah?" Sheen asked. "Well can you teach me to play ball? Maybe I can play for the Dodgers too."

The little boy chuckled and tossed the ball towards Sheen. Sheen caught it and tossed it around with the kids. Serena watched on from a distance and smiled. She loved seeing the way he easily interacted with the children. Though she could not help but wonder if this simple rite of passage, playing catch, was something Sheen had always wanted to do with his own son, but hadn't the opportunity.

One of the boys, a curious suspicion in his expression, watched Sheen. The detective realized that the child was reserved, not fully joining in the frivolity. The next time Sheen caught the ball, he lightly tossed it the young boy's way. The boy caught it, but kept his eyes on Sheen and didn't throw the ball towards anyone.

Just as Serena stepped up to the group, the young boy with the ball fought off his shyness and, in a voice that was embarrassed to speak up, asked Sheen, "How come you don't look like us?"

Serena couldn't be bothered by the uncomfortable moment. She was so touched that the introverted boy spoke up with such innocence and was moved by his childhood curiosity.

Sheen looked at the boy and asked, "Well, how come you don't look like me?" The boy shrugged his shoulders.

Sheen thoughtfully and playfully put his hand under his chin and considered the point for a moment. "Tell me... do you like hot dogs?"

"Yes," said the little boy.

"And hot fudge sundaes?"

"Yes."

"You seem like a good fella, so what difference does it make that we don't look alike?"

The boy considered this and said, "None, I guess."

"Agreed," Sheen asked. He stuck out his hand. The boy accepted his hand, they shook on it and the kid smiled a wide grin that showed a hole on his upper jaw where he'd recently lost a baby tooth. He tossed the ball in to Sheen and the play continued.

At Miami Stadium, the kids watched a double header. The first game featured the Little League City Champions, a team from West Flagler Park that was sponsored by Luby Chevrolet. One of their players had been injured in the championship game and this afternoon's matchup against a team of all-stars was to benefit the boy's medical bills. The second game was played by the Miami Sun Sox, in the middle of a very successful season where Billy Harris and Gil Torres were dominating on the pitcher's mound and the Sun Sox defense was superb.

Later that night, Sheen sat on his sofa, his arm around Serena as she rested her head on his shoulder. "That was nice today. You were so sweet with those children," Serena said.

Sheen nodded and replied, "It was fun."

"You were especially good with little Edward," Serena mentioned in reference to the boy with whom Sheen had discussed skin color.

"He's just a shy kid, he'll open up when given the chance." Sheen chuckled, "Reminds me of myself at that age, actually."

"It's more than shyness. Like he has no sense of belonging."

Sheen shrugged and responded, "Some people are beams of light in this world. Some are shadows. They don't always feel like they belong, or don't know how, so they stand in the back of the crowd, out of sight and off to the edge somewhere."

Serena thought on that as she snuggled closer to Sheen. Then she added, "Henrietta was always that beam of light. And I suppose I've always been a shadow. But that's fine, it suited the both of us that way."

"You said it yourself, you didn't know everything about your sister's life," Sheen said. "Maybe there was a part of her world where she was a shadow too."

Sheen's fingers intertwined with Serena's and he kissed her forehead.

Serena slept over again. Sheen was awoken by the sound of the ringing telephone. Though groggy, he was able to stumble his way towards the phone and answer it in just enough time to hear an irritated voice shout, "Sheen! Come get your pal!" Sheen could hear in the background, the boisterous singing of "Rule Britannia." He already knew what was going on.

After he'd hung up the phone, he stepped back into the bedroom and found that Serena was barely awake.

"I've got to go. A friend needs my help," Sheen said. "Will you be all right here alone?"

"Sure," she replied. "I've got Mr. Doyle to keep me company."

The bull terrier, hearing his name, raised his eyes and gave a disinterested look before laying his head down on his paws.

"I live alone, Ben. I'm used to it. Don't fret."

Sheen leaned across the bed and kissed Serena. "I'll be back, soon as I can." He walked out of the room and Serena turned over to reunite with her slumber.

⅄ ⅄ ⅄

Mickey Wails had been known to drink... and sometimes, too much. By the time Sheen got to Hannigan's Bar, Mickey had imbibed in far more than one too many. Fortunately, not much in the bar was destroyed. A bar stool, that Joe the barkeep knew Mickey would make good on, was the only property damage. Joe told Sheen about the evening's activities as Mickey quietly sang "Rule Britannia! Britannia rule the waves... La-la... never never never in the... U.S.A." The song became increasingly inaccurate and inappropriate as he went on.

Sheen draped Mickey's arm over his shoulder and nursed him to the car. Once he'd gotten Mickey in the passenger seat, Sheen lit up a Camel and got behind the wheel. He started the car and drove off.

"You want a cigarette, Mick?" Sheen asked.

"I do not," Mickey responded.

Sheen looked at his friend's condition and remarked, "You're gonna look like hell in the morning with that shiner."

"Ahhh..." Mickey waved off the comment with his hand and slurred, "Deserved it."

"What, you or the barstool?"

"The stool! Drinking with him all night, not one single word. Useless bastard." Mickey let out an uncontrollable, breathy laugh. As though he'd just said the funniest thing ever.

"Okay, Mick. What's it gonna be?" asked Sheen. "The drunk tank or my couch?"

"Your place. Drunk tank's not as hostipitle... hospitibibible..." Mickey gave up on the pronunciation and the slightest hiccup powered giggle escaped his throat before he observed, "That word's no fun right now."

After a few silent moments, Mickey was out. In his unconsciousness, his whole body dropped forward and his head smashed against the dashboard. Sheen merely shook his head and took another drag of his cigarette.

Sheen parked the car out in front of the house and helped Mickey stumble inside. As they entered the living room and Sheen switched on the light, Serena emerged from the hallway. Mickey saw her, surprised, not knowing who she was.

"Mickey, this is Serena Childress." Sheen explained, "Etta was her sister."

Mickey's shock was overtaken by the peculiarity of the situation and he let out a drunken, troubled laugh. "Wow." Mickey said, gesturing towards Serena and again at Sheen. "Okay." Even in his inebriated state, Mickey understood what was going on. He sat down on the couch and rested his head against the sofa's back.

Serena turned towards the hallway. Sheen stopped her by saying, "I'm sorry about that. He's drunk, obviously."

"Who is he?" Serena asked.

"My friend, Mickey. He's a good friend. He's been helping me with the case, actually."

Serena nodded then walked away.

Sheen turned his attention towards the drunken man on his sofa and helped position him so that he was lying comfortably. Sheen was about to turn out the light when he looked over at the cupboard. He reached inside the drawer, pulled out Matthew's picture and displayed it on one of the shelves.

He turned off the light and walked out of the room.

⋏ ⋏ ⋏

The next morning, Sheen was sitting at the table, reading the newspaper when Mickey slowly rolled over on the couch and sat up. He held his head, then noticed the pain on his cheek. He lightly touched it then flinched and said, "What happened to me last night?"

"You took on inanimate objects," replied Sheen. "In two places and twenty minutes apart."

Mickey got up on his feet and stretched, cracking his back in the process, then letting out an exhausted sigh.

"There's coffee," said Sheen.

Mickey moved towards the kitchen when Serena stepped into the room. The moment Mickey saw her he remembered his awkward reaction the night before, knowing enough to figure he might have offended her and his friend. "Miss. I am very sorry for the way I behaved last night. It's just that, when I saw you... well, I was taken a bit off-guard."

Serena nodded and said, "No apologies. You were drunk. I understand people say things they don't mean when they've been at the bottle."

"No ma'am," Mickey responded. "It's been my experience that people say exactly what they mean when they are drunk, only louder. They have the courage to do so. That's when you see everything honest about a person. Just magnified."

Mickey looked over at Sheen, a concerned expression on his face and said, "It doesn't matter to me, but the world is what it is. You two be careful." He turned and looked at Serena with apologetic eyes and said, "Again, Miss Childress. I'm sorry." Mickey extended his hand in friendship.

She smiled at him and said, "Serena." She took his hand, they shook and Mickey said, "A pleasure."

Serena sat across from Sheen as Mickey poured himself a cup of coffee. "So, where are you, then?" Mickey asked. "Any new information."

"I hope there will be today," Sheen answered. "I'm meeting a guy I know, could have something useful."

⅄ ⅄ ⅄

Detective Sheen stepped into the Trio Diner just past eleven thirty. Agent Levesque was already seated and smoking a cigarette that had no printing on it. Sheen approached the table, gestured at the cigarette between Levesque's fingers and remarked, "I see you still roll your own."

Levesque nodded, "It's therapeutic." Agent Richard Levesque was tall and lean, with a surprisingly round face that mismatched his thin body. His default expression was a jovial one, but when he turned his mind towards a problem, his concentration fashioned a scowl on his face.

The waitress approached the table and asked the two men to place their orders. Levesque spoke up and said, "Romanian steak and he'll have the same." The waitress wrote the order on a ticket and walked away. Levesque said to Sheen, "You're going to thank me. It's a skirt steak, they grill it with onions, it's delicious."

"Okay," Sheen accepted. "So, where are we with...?"

Levesque held up his hand to stop Sheen from continuing. "We'll enjoy our lunch, I'll leave and you will meet me at an apartment twenty minutes later. There you will look over the materials as I wait with you."

Sheen nodded, and after they'd finished their lunch, Agent Levesque paid the bill and left a folded piece of paper on the table. Levesque left the diner and Sheen unfolded the paper and saw an address had been written on it: 3694 SW 5th Terrace, Apartment 8C.

When Sheen arrived, he walked up the three floors of stairs to the apartment, knocked on the door, and found that Agent Levesque was there to answer. Levesque escorted Sheen into the room, and pointed to a file folder on a table. "That's what I've got for you. Take as much time as you need, but it can't go home with you."

The apartment was sparsely furnished. A table with two chairs near a kitchen that had a refrigerator and a small stove. Across the room was one sofa, big enough for two and a television set. Usually this apartment was for informants, witnesses under bureau protection, or a place for agents to stay in if needed.

Levesque left Sheen alone, sitting down on the sofa and relaxing for a few hours as he watched television. A rare moment of indulgence for the agent. Levesque knew he was blatantly breaking FBI protocol, by making the file available to his war buddy. But Levesque didn't agree with some of the tactics that his employers used and, after looking through the file himself, believed this woman to be nothing more than an acquaintance of a radical entertainer. These fringe personas that had no real threat of espionage or violence were, to him, scapegoats and cautionary tales. He felt his obligation to the man who saved his life was more important to him than giving away confidential information on some rabble-rousers.

Sheen sat at the table and looked through the file. He saw all the basic information on her date of birth, appearance and her occupational and residential facts. The file even had her physical measurements, which Sheen thought were probably not entirely difficult to attain through the professional world in which she inhabited, but he didn't truly understand their importance in the file.

Her association with Paul Robeson was also listed in great detail. Sheen suspected that this was probably the impetus for the bureau's initial investigation.

But then, something he hadn't previously known was listed. His eyes widened as he read the next portion of the file. A series of investigations, including stakeouts and tailing the subject's vehicle, revealed an unknown affair. The file's content confirmed that Henrietta Childress, AKA Etta Childs was romantically involved with Florida Governor Nathaniel Eldridge.

"Christ almighty," Sheen said under his breath. "Nate."

CHAPTER 12

ETTA CHILDS

Governor Nathaniel Eldridge was known as a man of the people. He had been throughout his entire political career, going back to his days as a district attorney and city councilman in Miami, all the way through his two terms as Miami mayor. His speeches often featured language painting pictures of hope and advancement for those who are willing to work hard and use their gifts to better their communities. He championed the working class and was considered to be as much of a candidate for the Negro vote as one could be in the South. Whenever the rights of black voters were not denied, many cast their vote for Eldridge. He had gained favor amongst the minority when he reached out to the Florida branch of the National Association for the Advancement of Colored People and assisted with the movement's actions to register new black voters. Some felt this was a genuine effort on Eldridge's part to display where he stood on civil rights issues, others believed it to be a political ploy to win over the few votes that black folks would be able to cast. Those who truly knew Eldridge realized that it was a combination of both motives.

His grandfather, Anson Eldridge, was the owner of a cotton plantation in the 1800's, and much of the labor done for his business was done by the slaves he owned that worked his fields. Rich enough to avoid the army, Anson did not take part in the battles of the Civil War. Instead, he became involved in the political battles of trying to protect the South from what he considered to be Northern intrusion on a way of life.

After the war his business remained afloat, despite having to now pay wages to his workers. It was during these years of reconstruction that Jacob Eldridge was born. When he came of age Jacob tried to make it in professional baseball, playing with the Jacksonville Jays, Macon Peaches and the Winston-Salem Blue Sluggers. He finally made a brief appearance in the major leagues playing for the Louisville Colonels of the National League. But he'd recently gotten engaged to a young woman from Valdosta that he'd met while playing for Macon. Upon the news that she was in the family way, they decided to return home to Jacob's father's cotton plantation, where he could work and eventually take over the company.

Just a few weeks after the new year of 1904 was ushered in, Jacob and his wife Vivian welcomed their son Nathaniel into the world. He grew up in an expanded empire, the Eldridge cotton business having grown much larger than it had been during the previous generation. More family money afforded Nathaniel with greater opportunities and coming of age between two world wars kept him out of military service. Both of these eventualities were factors in allowing Nathaniel to travel to Durham, North Carolina and attend Trinity College. By the time he graduated the school had been renamed Duke University. In addition to history and literature, Nathaniel also studied economics.

After his college career, Eldridge moved back to Florida, but chose to head south to Miami where he worked for the city council and married one of his aides, Mae Ellen Wurley. The two never had any children and were not able to enjoy a long marriage. Barely a year into their nuptials Mae Ellen was reported missing by a distraught

Nathaniel. She'd been gone for twenty-four days before her body was discovered in the Everglades. What was known was that she had been the victim of several violations before she was murdered. What was not known was the identity of her assailant.

Never one to wallow in self-pity, Nathaniel did not sink into depression. Though he did mourn his wife's passing and, in doing so, remained single for the next fifteen years. During that time he had been elected Mayor of Miami, and eventually the Governor of Florida.

⅄ ⅄ ⅄

One night in May of 1951, the tables at Copa City on Miami Beach were full, mostly with politicians and socialites, as the room delighted to the sound of Etta Childs singing "How High the Moon", "(What Did I Do to Be So) Black and Blue", and "Oh! Look at Me Now" accompanied by a top notch local jazz quintet.

The evening was a fundraiser for the Democratic party. During the course of the evening, Governor Nathaniel Eldridge would give a speech to the crowd and would make his way around the room, listening to the concerns of local civil servants as well as those with money to contribute that desired an audience with the Governor.

It was during Etta's sensuous performance of "How High the Moon" that she locked eyes with Nate. He had not been able to take his eyes off her since she stepped on the stage, but this was the first time she had noticed him. The rest of her performance was directed at one particular side of the room and it was the section that had the Governor's table.

Later in the evening, as the Governor made the rounds, he was guided to a table and the head of the Miami chapter of the Florida Democratic party, the gentleman who had arranged the fundraiser, said, "Governor Eldridge, I'd like you to meet Ms. Etta Childs who sang for us this evening."

Etta stood, smiled and stretched out her hand. Nate smiled back at her, shook her hand and said, "I'd like to thank you so much for performing for us this evening. You were just marvelous."

"Thank you, Governor," Etta replied.

"Are you very active with the party, Ms. Childs?"

"I have some issues that interest me, yes. Any in particular you feel I should know about, Governor?"

"Well we are making an aggressive push for a new law that uses the fees for licensing automobiles…"

Etta finished the Governor's sentence, "And spends it on education."

The Governor was impressed and his smile showed it as he said, "That's right."

"It was a frequent topic of conversation at a benefit I was at," she explained. "For Harry T. Moore. He's the director of the state's NAACP branch."

"I know Mr. Moore. He's a good man."

"Yes he is."

The local politician who'd introduced the two was now urging the Governor to move on as he placed a hand on Nate's back and said, "Sorry, sir. But there's a lot of folks still waiting to see you."

Nate nodded, smiled at Etta and said, "It's been a pleasure seeing you tonight."

"Thank you. It was lovely meeting you, sir."

Before Nate could enjoy saying goodbye, he was whisked over to another table. Etta watched him as he left and kept her gaze on him as he spoke to another group of financiers.

Jonah Fisk had spent most of his evening standing near the entrance to the main room at Copa City. His keen eye had been on the Governor all night, as it was his job to do so, being the lead man on Eldridge's protection detail. He hadn't gotten much of an opportunity to eat anything other than some canapés that had been offered him from a tray going back towards the kitchen. Once the event had begun to shut down and Governor Eldridge had chosen to speak to his Chief of Staff, Jensen Stone, in the safe haven of the club's kitchen, Jonah finally got the opportunity to have some food. He had taken one of the cooks up on their offer to make him a corned beef sandwich.

Stone and the Governor had been discussing one of the points of legislation brought up earlier by one of the constituents when Jonah took the final bite of his potato pancake. It was just at that moment, after Stone had exited the kitchen, that the Governor walked up to Jonah and asked, "That singer that was here tonight... Ms. Childs. Would you see if she's still here and if she would be interested in continuing our conversation?"

Fisk was caught off guard by the request. It was rare for the Governor to send Fisk on a quiet errand to arrange a meeting with someone after an event, but it had happened a few times during the two years he had worked for Eldridge. Usually it occurred when the Governor felt he hadn't given someone enough of his time to discuss their issue, or if Eldridge found someone particularly interesting and wanted to spend more time with them. Jonah saw the look in Eldridge's eyes and realized that the Governor was interested in Ms. Childs on a number of levels.

Fisk's job was protecting the Governor and serving his requests. This was a request, no matter what Fisk thought of it and it wasn't his concern to say no. He nodded his head and dutifully said, "Yes, sir."

Fifteen minutes later, when Jonah lead the Governor out of the kitchen, he informed the Governor that the main room was empty, except for Ms. Childs and she was delighted to stay behind and meet with him. Eldridge entered the room and saw Etta sitting at one of the tables all the way on the other side of the club. She stood, but sat down again after he smiled and gestured with his hands for her to stay put. Etta found that to be the act of a gentleman.

"Thank you for staying, Ms. Childs," Eldridge said.

"I'm happy to," she responded.

Nate took her hand and kissed it before he sat down. "Mr. Moore of the NAACP. We were discussing him before I was ushered off."

"Yes, sir."

"He's been involved in trying to appeal the convictions in the case of what happened in Groveland a few years back. I'm sure you know all about that."

"Mm-hmmm," Etta replied. She'd kept an eye on the developments following the trial, wherein a number of black men had been accused of raping a white woman. But the truth of the situation was largely unknown and many believed the men had been falsely accused and wrongly convicted.

"It's difficult to know what happened there, but the law is the law and burden of proof is supposed to mean something," Nate said. Etta didn't say much, she just sort of bobbed her head slowly, not fully committed to agreeing with him. Then he asked, "What do you think?"

Etta looked up and pursed her lips, genuinely giving it the due consideration then responded, "When I was just a young thing, waiting tables back home, there was a young man got murdered by white folks for something that no one should ever be killed over. And I remember my Mother said to me 'Our peoples is born grieving'." Etta thought on that for a moment, keeping her stare directly on

Nate and then she shook her head and added, "But we shouldn't be. No one should."

Nate nodded and replied, "I can respect that point of view."

"And I don't think you came here to talk to me about politics," Etta added.

Nate smiled, knowing he was caught.

"You just don't know how to tell me the things you want to tell me," Etta accurately pointed out.

"You're right, I don't," Nate responded.

"Say it the way you would say it to anyone else."

Nate smiled, enchanted by her forthcoming ways, and told her, "I've been captivated by you since the moment I watched you on that stage. And it hasn't gone away all night. You're remarkable and I think you're the most beautiful woman I've ever met."

"That wasn't so hard, was it?"

Nate laughed, almost a boyish giggle. Etta knew he was nervous and so was she. But her nerves were cooled by the fact that she could control the situation.

"You stood out in the crowd tonight," Etta confessed. "And not because you're the Governor. I mean you stood out for me. I looked around this room and saw what I always see when I'm on-stage. Admiration, enjoyment, lust... but you were looking into my eyes, truly looking into them. I saw a man who fell for a woman. It's the same look I see right now."

Etta's stare became intense and she was sharing a genuine moment, one between a performer and a politician, neither of whom got to experience many moments without an angle, some collection of strings attached. Both felt they weren't the designation of their careers or respective stars in their individual vocations. They were a man attracted to a woman and a woman who felt the same way.

"You want to kiss me, don't you?" Etta asked.

"Yes," Nate replied with a painful longing.

"I want you to."

Nate thought for a moment, leaned in, then slightly turned his head to look over his shoulder. But before he could view the surrounding area Etta grabbed his chin and turned his face towards her.

"No one else is here and if you want to kiss me there is only one thing you should do right now."

Nate didn't need further invitation. He moved towards her, placed his lips against hers. Etta opened her mouth slightly and let his bottom lip enter her mouth. They shared a kiss that was sensuous but gave way before it reached a higher level of passion.

After the kiss ended, neither moved away and their eyes were locked in a stare, a smile creeping across Etta's face. Nate exhaled, relief after so many years without romance, understanding how much he missed companionship. He felt as though Etta was the woman he'd needed to meet at this time in his life, someone who could get under his skin in the best ways possible that he would never want to shake.

They spent the better part of an hour talking, both a little bit about their pasts and quite a bit about their current lives of much renown. Etta and Nate each came away from the conversation realizing that it's true what so many before them had said: It's lonely at the top. But both of them quietly suspected that maybe the best way to cope with that loneliness was to spend time with someone else that understood that particular condition.

⅄ ⅄ ⅄

"I fall in love too easily, I fall in love too fast" were the final lyrics sung in Etta Childs' performance at the Miami Beach Municipal Auditorium, which Governor Eldridge attended a little more than a month later.

It was Jonah Fisk's job to discreetly collect Etta three hours after the performance, drive her to the hotel that Nate was staying at, bring her through the service entrance and quietly get on an elevator with her before leading her to the Governor's room.

That night, Etta and Nate became physically intimate for the first time in their relationship. Nate had never been with a woman of color before. This wasn't the first time Etta had dated outside of her race. She had made it with a few Latin gentlemen in Hollywood and once spent a few weeks seeing a handsome Greek fellow during a month-long engagement in Paris. But she'd never gotten involved with a white man until now.

The first night they made love twice. The next night, they only did it once, but slept in each other's arms for several hours before Etta had to sneak out of the building.

As their romance became more passionate, it became more difficult for Jonah to make the arrangements. Particularly when Etta would come to visit Nate in Tallahassee. For quite some time, they had agreed she should not come to the capital to spend time with him. But the deeper they fell in love, the more they realized it was impossible to be apart for too long a time, and Eldridge was primarily in Tallahassee.

When Nate mentioned to Jonah that Etta was going to be in town and he wanted his guard to set it up so they could meet, the Governor saw a reaction of disappointment for the first time ever from his employee.

"You don't like the idea of me and her, do you?" Nate asked.

Jonah held his tongue for a moment, then said, "I work for you, sir. I don't have an opinion. It certainly isn't my place, Governor."

"I want you to speak freely. I trust you with this job and I want to clear the air. I'd feel better that way, Jonah."

"Sir, I'm from the South. Born and raised in Mississippi, lived down here all my life."

"I'm the grandson of a slave-owning plantation master, the farthest North I've ever been is D.C. I know what it is to come from the South, Mr. Fisk. You think what I'm doing is unnatural. It bothers you, doesn't it?"

Jonah thought about what the Governor had said about clearing the air, and felt that he wouldn't get out of this conversation if he wasn't candid. So he responded, "Yes, it does. Blacks and whites... that just shouldn't be. It's an awful thing, sir. And it makes it harder on all of us that are around you, to have to keep your secrets. I think it's just damn foolish. Still, you needn't feel like we need to clear the air for me to do my job. Trust in the fact that I am here for what you need, no matter what."

Jonah let that sit between them for a moment, then added, "Anyway, I work for you, sir. I don't have an opinion."

That was the last real conversation of any conflict that Nate ever had with Jonah. The Governor continued to see Etta, and Jonah continued to arrange it and protect the couple's privacy.

The next moment of controversy that Nate faced was when he had to come clean on the relationship with his top advisor and chief of staff, Jensen Stone. One evening, several months into the relationship, Stone asked Jonah to have the Governor meet him at one of their favorite restaurants in Tallahassee that served pulled pork sandwiches with spicy coleslaw. Jonah hesitated, knowing that Nate had plans to meet Etta that evening. "Okay, sir," Jonah said after a pause, "I'll just run it by the Governor."

Jensen furrowed his brow and gave Fisk a sideways look, asking the bodyguard, "What's the problem? Does the Governor have plans I don't know about?"

"I just need to check with him, that's all," Jonah responded, trying to not let the cat out of the bag.

But Stone was insistent and went to Nate's office. He explained about the plans to go for sandwiches and discuss a few governmental matters over dinner. Nate's face registered disappointment and Stone read it. He asked, "What? What's the problem? You've got other plans, tell me what they are."

"I," Nate stopped himself and choked back a sigh. A frustrated breath pushed out through his nose. He looked over Stone's shoulder and saw Jonah standing in the doorway. For a moment the Governor was almost asking for help, but he realized Jonah didn't have any answers for him either.

Stone followed Nate's stare and turned to look back at Jonah. He could see on Jonah's face that there was information the two shared that he wasn't privy to.

"What don't I know that I should?" Stone asked.

"I've been seeing someone," Nate confessed.

Stone smiled, pleased to hear the news and responded, "That's great. Who is she?"

Nate didn't know how to answer the question, so as directly as possible he simply uttered, "Etta Childs."

Puzzled, Stone thought about it and mentioned, "I know that name."

"She performed at the fundraiser in Miami earlier this year. Also I attended one of her shows on Miami Beach."

Stone's face turned. Shock and concern were blended with a hint of anger and he said, "That's not possible. Because that was a colored woman that performed at those events and the Governor of the state of Florida can't have an inappropriate relationship with a Negro. Now why don't you tell me who the hell you're really talking about!"

"I'm seeing Etta Childs."

"Jesus Christ, Nathaniel! You son of a bitch. That's God damned ridiculous!" Stone turned to look at Jonah and questioned him with, "And you knew all about this?"

Stone raised a pair of pleading hands, outstretched at his sides as if to finish the sentence by gesturing 'and you didn't tell me?' Jonah clearly picked up on the body language because he responded, "I work for the Governor, sir."

"Well, that's *fantastic*," Stone exclaimed! He turned his attention to Nate and said, "What do you think is going to happen when this comes out? How long do you think this is going to be a secret only to the people in this room?"

"It's already been eight months, so who's to say..."

"Eight months?" Stone shouted!

"It does not matter! Whatever comes my way, comes my way! We're going to protect this. *You're* going to protect this! I'm not just pushing her aside, I love her!"

Jonah heard the words for the first time and closed his eyes. He knew it was possible that this is where it had gone, but now it hit him like a ton of bricks.

Stone was equally shocked. He couldn't force words out of his open mouth, but his gaze went off in the distance. What a disaster, he thought. "Sir, I don't know what to do in this situation. I feel like I can advise you on anything, but this... I just don't know."

"We are going to keep doing what we're doing," Nate said.

"If it's revealed, it'll ruin you," Stone replied.

"Then let's not let it be revealed."

Stone nodded, concerned but powerless, and asked, "Is there anything I can do to add more security, more protection for..."

"I don't know, ask Jonah. He's been handling it."

Jonah interjected, "I'll be fine, Mr. Stone."

"Okay... okay." Stone's surprise was still new and he couldn't argue the point. He knew how Nathaniel was when he was passionate about something, that's one of the reason's he'd wanted to get him elected in the first place. Now it was the passion for a woman and history had proven that there is no way to combat that.

"Thank you, Governor," Jensen said as he walked towards the door.

"Good night," Nate said.

⅄ ⅄ ⅄

The last three months that Etta and Nate spent together were some of the best times either had experienced in their lives. They fought occasionally, but Etta liked that they did. It made her feel like they were just as normal as any other couple that went through their difficult times. But they frequently made love, and although they had to live their romance in secrecy, they found ways to have dinners and the occasional picnic together.

Most of her life, Etta had found pleasure in the excitement she gave others. With Nate, she loved the reciprocation of their relationship, that she enjoyed feeling good about it for herself as much as she enjoyed pleasing her lover. So many people in her life knew Henrietta Childress and the others knew Etta Childs. Nate was the first person she ever knew where she felt like Etta and Henrietta could be the same person.

Etta firmly believed that she would not live to see a day where two people in this taboo sort of relationship could publicly be with each other, let alone be married. But that didn't change the simple fact that Etta was deeply in love with Nate and wanted to spend the rest of her life with him.

CHAPTER 13

THE WIND KNOCKED OUT

Mickey walked through the doorway and already he was animated in one-way conversation. "Incredible," he said. "Never in all my years, *never* seen anything like it. Sugar Ray had Maxim down on all the judge's scorecards, but the heat just killed him."

Mickey didn't even notice Sheen sitting next to his dining table, completely dazed, shocked and in a world of his own thought.

"They had to replace the referee, Yankee Stadium was so damn hot. And then like nothing, Robinson just passes out. The news said it was a hundred and three degrees in the ring." Mickey shook his head and sighed in disbelief. Then for the first time he really looked at Sheen and noticed his friend was stunned.

"Hey, Ben. I know it was unbelievable, nobody would've ever thought Robinson would endure his first knockout that way, but," Mickey shrugged and continued, "you know, it's just a fight."

Sheen looked up, met Mickey's eyes with his own, then furrowed his brow with great concern.

"What is it, pal?" Mickey asked.

"I know who Nate is," Sheen responded. He still wished the truth was not what it was, but no amount of discomfort would change the facts.

Mickey sat down across from Sheen. Ben poured both of them a glass of whiskey and he reported the news of Etta and Governor Eldridge to his associate. Mickey's surprise equaled Sheen's by the time the story had been finished.

After sitting in silence for a few minutes, Mickey concluded with no amount of certainty, "I don't know, Ben. I think you need to tell them. I don't really know everything that's going on here with you and Serena Childress, but I know what I've seen and that leads me to believe it's somewhat serious. So you need to tell her. And Wendell Childress... well, he's your client, Ben. Is there any reason you can think of that you shouldn't tell him?"

Sheen shrugged his shoulders, unable to think of one and said, "No. Not that I know of." He poured himself another shot of whiskey and exhaled a disturbed and frustrated sigh.

人 人 人

Sheen had called both Serena and Wendell and had told them that he had new information that would be difficult to hear, but important to the investigation. It had been suggested that Sheen join them at Wendell's house in Richmond Heights for a barbecue on Sunday afternoon.

As Sheen drove through the Richmond Heights neighborhood, he was impressed by the sheer amount of houses that had been built and were occupied. Easily hundreds of homes existed in this ever expanding section of town. A large water tower overlooked acres of well-built, solid houses, evenly placed in close proximity to one another. This was definitely a community where you got to know your neighbor very well, practically sharing your yard on either side with them. However close the houses were to each other it did seem that each homeowner had plenty of space. Behind the houses, one backyard seemed to blend with that of the home behind it.

When Sheen pulled up to the address he'd been given as Wendell's, he saw that Serena was already there. She was sitting on the front stoop, her young niece in her lap, in a rocking chair that matched the one to her left, occupied by Wendell's wife, Pearl.

Serena was plain looking on this day, wearing a summer dress she'd borrowed from Pearl's closet. Earlier in the day Serena had on her Sunday best as she accompanied the rest of the Childress family to Bethel Baptist Church. What Sheen could not shake from his mind, as he approached the ladies on the front porch, was how he was just as enamored with Serena in her "dressed-down" state as in any of the other instances he'd seen and spent time with her.

"Good afternoon, Ben," Serena said with a smile that bordered on giving too much away to the others around.

"Hello. How are you?" Ben asked.

"Very fine, thank you." Serena gestured towards her sister-in-law and said, "This is Pearl. Wendell's wife."

They shook hands and Pearl said, "Very nice to meet you, Detective Sheen."

"It's my pleasure, ma'am," he replied.

Serena kissed the cheek of the three-year old girl she held in her lap and said, "And this is little Althea."

"Well, hello there," Sheen said.

The shy little girl spoke in a delicate manner, saying, "Hello, sir."

Serena chuckled. Sheen smiled and remarked, "She's a little angel."

"Thank you," responded Pearl.

Serena nodded her head at the side of the house and explained, "Wendell's out around back. We'll come and join you in a little while."

"Terrific," Sheen said and smiled once more at the little girl who had already moved on to focusing on the grasshopper leaping up and down on the front yard. Ben walked away and headed towards the backyard.

When Sheen approached Wendell, his client was standing in front of a Weber-Stephen's kettle grill, slathering red sauce on pork ribs and chicken.

"Afternoon, Mr. Childress," Sheen said as he extended his hand. Childress placed the round cover on the grill, wiped his right hand on the towel he had hanging from a belt loop on his pants and shook Sheen's hand.

"Detective. Welcome to my home."

"Thank you. It's very pleasant."

Wendell looked around his property with pride, taking in the hedges and plants he had landscaped himself and smiled, "Yes sir, it's a good home."

Sheen enjoyed the meal with Wendell, Serena and their family. Quite some time after they'd finished eating the barbecue that Wendell had masterfully prepared, Wendell sat in the backyard smoking a cigar while Sheen sat next to him enjoying one of his Camels. Serena had gone into the kitchen to help Pearl fix some coffee and dish up the blueberry cobbler that Mrs. Childress had made.

Eyeing Wendell as he smoked, Sheen inquired, "Mr. Childress, what do you think of Governor Eldridge?"

Wendell shrugged, puffed on his stogie and replied, "Ain't give him much thought, tell you the truth".

Sheen nodded then asked, "You vote?"

"No." Wendell turned his head towards Sheen. "Listen here," Wendell stated and paused long enough to let Sheen know the weight of what he was about to say. "We got the right to vote as an idea. But action, that's a different kinda thing. S'posin' I was gonna vote for that man, or any man, I ain't necessarily guaranteed that right on any particular day. And that's just somethin' that goes on if'n you ain't white. Now you gotta know that."

"Certainly wouldn't surprise me," Sheen responded.

"Mm-hmm", Wendell took another puff off his cigar. "I come back from the war, fought for this country, but I ain't wavin' it's flag. Plenty places I ain't welcome, plenty things when I came back ain't no different just 'cause I served. This here, low income housing they built for other veterans that look like me, one of the few good deals they got. But most of them rights, they make 'em for you, Detective. Not me. If that ain't truth, then grits ain't groceries."

Sheen didn't know how to respond. He wasn't going to apologize, because what would Wendell be able to do with that? And he felt sanctimonious trying to claim all the white man's evils that had for generations become the black man's burden. Instead he just listened and nodded his head, the best form of empathy he could provide.

"I ain't sayin' this to give you a hard time," Wendell continued, "and I sure ain't tellin' you for want of pity. I'm just sayin' that what is, is what is."

"I guess all your enemies weren't survived in the war."

"I ain't got no use for enemies. Life is hard enough to need all that grief. I ain't tryin' to fight with no one."

"So what's your philosophy on the people in this world that are against you?"

Wendell shrugged and said, "Hell with 'em... I'll outlive 'em."

Sheen chuckled, he liked that approach. Not only that, but he liked Wendell. This is a good man, trying to earn his daily bread and get through life with as little hassle as the rest of us, he thought.

Once the ladies had returned with coffee and dessert, Sheen felt it was time he let the cat out of the bag in regards to his latest discovery about Henrietta's life.

"Listen, there's something I've uncovered during my investigation and... it may be troubling to you. It's certainly going to take some time to accept," Sheen explained.

"You go on ahead and say what you got to," Wendell said as he squeezed his wife's hand. "The three of us is family here, so you can speak plain, Detective".

Serena took in a breath, preparing for what she sensed might be shocking news.

"See the thing of it is..." Sheen grimaced, then forced himself to be the uncomfortable messenger. "I've learned who Nate is. Henrietta was involved, romantically, with... uh... Nathaniel Eldridge. As in Governor Eldridge."

Sheen couldn't look them in the eye at first, feeling the surrounding awkwardness. Serena was shocked, not so much disappointed. Pearl's shock was more dramatic, but Wendell was the only one whose shock was coupled with anger.

"You know this?" he demanded! "This is certain?"

"Yes, sir," Sheen replied. "I'm positive that it is. Right now, that's all I am sure of. Whether this relationship has anything to do with her murder, I don't know. But they did have a relationship that was kept secret."

"And was damned foolish," Wendell exclaimed! "Two people like that got no business carryin' on together."

Serena batted her eyes, nervous about Wendell's reaction to this revelation, particularly considering her own recent love life.

"It's just plain stupid to do somethin' like that," Wendell added. He shot a stern look in Serena's direction. Wendell had no idea what was going on between the detective and his sister, but he'd caught enough pleasant glances between the both of them to be concerned.

"I'm sorry for the shock," Sheen offered. "Later on this week I'll be traveling to Tallahassee. I'm going to seek an audience with the Governor and ask him whatever questions I can get away with. In the meantime, perhaps it's best to keep this quiet amongst yourselves."

"Oh, believe me, we got no call to let others know anything about this," Wendell griped.

Serena was silent, biting her lip and contemplating her brother's reaction. Sheen also felt sheepish about the whole thing, sitting in an awkward silence.

⊥ ⊥ ⊥

Big City Blues, the final picture of Etta Childs' career, would be released months after her death. Serena Childress had asked Ben Sheen to go to the movie house and see it with her. Sheen was thrilled to be asked, thinking that this would be sort of a date... or the closest thing to a real date that they had experienced.

As they drove to the theater, they danced around the subject of Wendell's reaction at the barbecue. Had they directly and honestly discussed it, both would have revealed that it was a difficult thing to cope with, but neither thought of ending their whirlwind romance. And neither would accept that as a solution. They enjoyed being with each other far too much and felt like they ultimately had to decide for themselves what was best.

But they didn't discuss the matter in such great detail, rather shrugging off Wendell's reaction, both admitting they understood it, but neither wanting to make things messy.

Instead, Sheen went deeper into the romance, asking Serena about her family and life in Miami. At one point he asked a question that had interested him for weeks.

"Why does Wendell call you Sesa?"

Serena smiled, pleased that he wanted to know. "When he was younger, Wendell used to mix up his words something awful and he would stutter," Serena explained. "He couldn't read very well either. A man who went to our church that was a professor, he told Mama that Wendell had difficulty thinking about words and communicating sometimes because of it. We finally learned that when he would call me Sesa, it was because he would mix up Serena and sister in his thoughts and it would come out wrong. At first we used to laugh about it, tease him a little. Then we understood it was hard on him so we stopped. Finally he stopped stuttering, his reading got better and he didn't mix words up anymore. But even after he could say my name proper, he would still call me Sesa. He just... " Serena smiled and thought fondly of it as she explained, "I guess it just became his own nickname for me."

When they arrived at the theater, they agreed that they should walk in separately and that Sheen would wait until the lights went down to walk to the seats.

"I'll find a couple of seats in the back," Serena said.

Minutes later, in a darkened movie theater, Sheen sat down next to Serena and they enjoyed a few hours of being out on a date. Sheen even reached over and held Serena's hand as they watched Etta's final film performance as the female lead, of a mostly black cast, in a movie about a New York jazz club run by a group of numbers-running gangsters.

Before the lights came up, as the final cast credits were being shown, Sheen stood up and walked out of the theater. Moments later, Serena exited through the lobby and reconvened with Ben around the corner.

They got into Sheen's Coupe and he drove to his house with her head rested on his shoulder as Ella Fitzgerald sang along with Benny Goodman's arrangement of *Goodnight My Love*

.

CHAPTER 14

TRUTH TO POWER

S heen reached into the kitchen drawer and pulled out a cast iron combination bottle and beer can opener. It had the words "Dixie Beer Co." on it. The tool was a novelty, shaped to have the pointed can opener end of it fashioned after the head of an axe. He'd picked it up years earlier while travelling through New Orleans, where the Dixie Brewing Company was based. But on this night he used the opener to puncture the top of a can of Schlitz. He moved towards the living room, taking a seat on the couch as he swallowed his first sip of the "beer that made Milwaukee famous".

Sheen was tired and his head was full of too many questions. Wondering about the Governor's involvement with Etta Childs and his own nerves of having to ask this man questions of that nature. He was also concerned with the way this revelation had been received by Wendell, particularly since Sheen was now deeply involved with the man's sister.

Sheen sat back, comfortably resting his head against the top of the sofa. He closed his eyes, resting them for a moment as he tried to relax.

He opened them as he heard a key jostling the lock on the door. He looked over at the front entrance and saw the deadbolt turn. As he did he quickly thought, "Mickey doesn't have a key? Who the hell... ?" His question was answered before he could fully ponder it as the door swung open and he saw Opal.

It had been years since Sheen had seen his wife, but there Opal stood, a suitcase at her feet and what appeared to be a tattered kit bag slung over her shoulder. She was haggard, dingy, and the smile on her face seemed forced. If she didn't have a nice piece of luggage beside her she could easily be mistaken for a hobo.

Before Sheen could say hello or ask her anything, Opal began to scream, uncontrollably and in astonishing terror. Her eyes locked on something across the room. Sheen followed her gaze and it directed his eyes towards the entry of the hallway. Standing in confusion at the stranger who stood by the door was Serena.

Sheen immediately went towards Opal and explained, "No no no, it's fine. Don't worry."

Opal backed away from Sheen as he got closer. Trying to explain, Sheen got louder and exclaimed, "Opal, listen to me!"

His wife cowered in the corner, her screams turning to whimpers, crying as she shook, afraid of being forcibly silenced. Her reaction confused Sheen as he stared at her and said, "It's all right."

"Is it?" asked a deep and familiar voice that Sheen reacted to, turning his head and looking across the room to find Wendell. Sheen was shocked to see him but more confused as he saw Wendell using a butcher's knife to cut raw beef off the bone on a chopping block he'd set on Sheen's table. Wendell looked down his nose at Sheen as he carved another slice.

Sheen's confusion was enhanced by the fact that, not only was Wendell suddenly gone, but now Sheen sat at the table where he'd just been. And now Governor Eldridge was sitting across from him, puffing on a cigar. "It's a bad idea, buddy," Eldridge said. "Take it from a man who knows."

Sheen looked down at the table in front of him and saw three playing cards in his hand and four face-up cards on the table. Eldridge also had cards and a variety of poker chips were strewn about the table. Eldridge grabbed a fistful of chips and tossed them on the table and...

Sheen woke up, sweat on his brow, confusion mapped all over his face.

⅄ ⅄ ⅄

Sheen hadn't bothered to go back to sleep. He had woken from his dream at a little after 4:30 am and he had a six o'clock train to catch. After boarding the "Dixie Flagler" train at the downtown station, he sat in his seat and stared out the window. The train was jointly operated by the Florida East Coast Railroad, the Pennsylvania Railroad, the Atlantic Coast Line Railroad and the Louisville and Nashville Railroad. Sheen would take the train to Jacksonville, where he would then board a train on the Florida Central and Western Railroad line that would eventually get him to Tallahassee.

By the time he would reach the state's capital, it would be too late in the afternoon to meet with the Governor. Especially since he had to use his brief contact with Josh Riley to access Eldridge, and talking Riley into the meeting had to come first.

Once he arrived, he stopped at a local coffee shop near the station for a grilled cheese on rye and a bowl of tomato soup. Then he checked into a cheap motel and got a good night's rest.

The next morning he made the trip by taxi cab to the state house. He asked to see Josh Riley and the receptionist called Riley at his office. The name Benjamin Sheen rang a bell in Riley's mind, but he wasn't sure why.

"What is this in regards to, sir?" the receptionist asked.

Sheen replied, "Just tell him I'm the Miami detective that called him several weeks ago about the Etta Childs matter."

Once the receptionist reported that information, Riley enthusiastically recalled and instructed the woman to send Sheen to his office.

"Nice set up," Sheen said as he entered Riley's office. "I'm guessing it beats a desk in the Miami News room."

Riley smiled and responded, "They've done well by me, given me a place to do what I do." They shook hands and Riley gestured towards the chair in front of his desk, which Sheen sat in.

"What brings you around, Detective? You're certainly far from home".

"I am. But, I need your help with something. I need to speak privately with Governor Eldridge."

Riley's eyes widened, not expecting that kind of request. Before Josh could respond, Sheen added, "I realize it's a big thing I'm asking. After all, we don't really know each other that well, but I assure it's important. And it concerns you in as much as you'd asked me to keep you apprised of the investigation."

"I did, but why the Governor? I'm sure you can understand my confusion," Riley responded.

Sheen nodded, then looked over his shoulder at the open door to the office. He looked back at Riley, stood up and pointed at the doorway. "Do you mind if I... ?"

"No, go ahead."

Sheen closed the door and took his seat across from Riley.

"Mr. Riley," Sheen began, "What I'm going to tell you is very sensitive but it's absolutely crucial to what I'm trying to learn about Etta Childs. It is also absolutely the truth."

"Okay," Riley responded with a curious yet already unsettled manner.

"Governor Eldridge and Etta Childs were carrying on in a romantic relationship that lasted for the better part of the past year. And, as far as I know, it lasted up until the day she died."

Riley's reaction wasn't dramatic, but it was one of great surprise as he simply and directly stated, "My God."

Sheen gave Riley a few moments to digest the truth of the matter, then proceeded to make his plea. "Thing of it is, I don't really know what the full extent of the Governor's involvement is, and I promise you that I'm not assuming anything here. But I do need some answers, at the very least I need to see if his responses can lead me down a further path. As I said, I know this is a great favor to ask of someone I hardly know... but I think it's the right thing to do. I think for someone to answer for Ms. Child's, I have to talk to the Governor."

Riley was already in agreement as he slowly nodded his head. After a few moments of concern on his face and a world of thoughts crowding his brain, he said, "Yes. I agree with you. Let me see what I can do."

"Thank you," Sheen said.

⅄ ⅄ ⅄

Governor Eldridge had received the call from Riley about twenty minutes to twelve. He had double-checked with Jonah Fisk, one of the few men who knew about him and Etta, regarding Jensen Stone's schedule. Stone being one of the others that was aware of the Governor's romantic trysts. Fisk had let Eldridge know that his chief of staff was having a lunch meeting with men from the state treasury office to discuss the budget. Eldridge found that to be perfect timing, as he didn't want Stone to know he was meeting with this detective from Miami. The Governor knew that Jensen would immediately assess the political ramifications of the scenario and that he'd try to keep the detective as far away from Eldridge as possible. But Nate, thinking about Etta, whom he had truly loved, felt he needed to talk to this man.

The introduction was awkward as Riley brought Sheen into the Governor's office. Riley had not had much time at all to swallow the new information about his boss's love life. And Eldridge had kept this secret amongst three people for so long that being in the room with two others that knew the truth was quite strange.

The awkwardness did not lessen after Riley was asked to step out and Eldridge spoke with this stranger who had uncovered the relationship for what it was.

"Detective, how did you find out?" Eldridge bluntly asked.

"This is what I do, Governor," Sheen tried to get away with that simple response. But the look on Nate's face was not going to allow something that simple.

Sheen offered a little bit more, "The name Nate came up a number of times in my investigation, from several people I talked to. After that, I was given information that pointed to your seeing Ms. Childs. I can assure you that nobody you trust gave this information if that's what worries you."

"That leads me to believe I'm under some sort of official investigation by someone other than a Miami private detective."

"I honestly don't know that, sir. But Etta was and that's as far as I can go with that information, Governor."

"Fair enough. So what is it you hope to accomplish here today, Detective?"

"Truth be told, I'm not really sure. But seeing as you were as close to her as anyone in her last months of life, perhaps you can fill me in on some things. Any trouble she had with another person? Frankly, I'm trying to find a legitimate suspect I can point the finger at."

"Detective, I hope this isn't your clever way of trying to point that finger in my direction."

"Honestly, I don't know either way. But Etta had a big secret and that secret was you."

"I loved Henrietta, Detective. She was the most beautiful woman I've ever known and that includes my dearly departed wife. And if you think it's easy for me to admit that I loved Etta more than the woman I married and grieved for, then you are sorely mistaken. Now I agreed to meet with you today because I want to know what happened to her and I'm hoping you have got something that can help you find that out. But I am going to say this to you one time and hope you understand the full weight of the Governor of your state discussing accusations of murder... I did not kill Etta Childs. I couldn't do that and I never would."

Sheen nodded, "Thank you, sir. I appreciate you saying that and I appreciate the... as you put it, weight of the situation."

Eldridge nodded, accepting that they now had a mutual understanding. He sat back and relaxed a little bit as their conversation continued.

"How long did this relationship last?"

"How is that important?"

"It's just that the longer a relationship like this is, the more intimate it is. The more you would actually talk to each other... to be blunt, sir, the less it would just be a sexual relationship."

"What we had was not tawdry, Detective," Eldridge snapped back. That was the moment that Sheen was convinced... the direct speech that Eldridge made about not killing Etta didn't really amount to much for Sheen. He felt that this was a politician, it's his job to sound honest whether he was or not. But in this moment, Eldridge's reaction to Sheen's explanation, that was honest. Nate was angered by the fact that Sheen cheapened, even for a brief moment, the connection he had with Etta. Sheen knew that Governor Eldridge was not her killer.

"We talked quite a lot," Eldridge confessed. "About any number of things. Like a real relationship. That wasn't usual for either of us. In my business, and in hers, there's a lot that simply isn't genuine. Even in your basic relationships. But with her I could be honest, and she with me."

"Did she mention anyone she knew, people she was maybe scared of or upset with? Someone who was upset with her?"

"She had a boxer friend, a local boy that was smitten with her. She knew he wanted to date her, but she was with me and she was happy. She talked to him a lot, he was a sympathetic ear. She knew that played on his emotions for her and she felt a little guilty about that, which I thought was very sweet."

Clete Tompkins, Sheen thought. But Tompkins was in no way a suspect, Sheen had ruled him out, much for the same reasons he had just eliminated Eldridge.

"There was a producer, I don't recall his name, but he was working on her last picture that she'd made. The two of them butted heads a bit, creative differences I think."

"Do you remember what the arguments were about, specifically?"

"Something about the way she was depicted in one scene. She told him that it wasn't a Hollywood movie and that they needed to be respectful of the community. She said he was trying to make it into a minstrel show."

"Was this a white man?"

"Yes. But he wasn't really in the movie business, at least not yet. He had put up the money for the thing and he was trying to get his foot in the door. But the picture's director was black and so were most of the other people working on the show. Listen, I'll be honest with you, I didn't always understand her point of view on things.

Especially when it came to race issues. But this was an argument over a movie role and this producer probably took the position that she was uppity. But that hardly seems like reason to seek her out and kill her, don't you think?"

Sheen agreed with Eldridge and the Governor offered no further ideas on possible suspects. He also admitted to not having seen Etta for three weeks before her passing and that last time they were together she hadn't seem troubled, nor did she mention anyone that she'd had a problem with at the time.

Finally the Governor suggested, "Have you considered the possibility that this was a random act of violence? A robbery or just some perverted, disturbed person wanting to kill someone and Etta was in the wrong place at the wrong time?"

"She was strangled, Governor," Sheen stated. "Not only did she let the person into her home, but they strangled her. Gunshots are random, knives are sadistic. Strangling someone is personal. You strangle someone, it's because you want to take their last breath with your hands."

⅄ ⅄ ⅄

Jensen Stone returned from his lunchtime meeting, which had not lasted nearly as long as expected. He walked past the Governor's office just in time to see Detective Sheen exit and to see Josh Riley escort him away. Stone didn't recognize Sheen, but that wasn't his major concern. What he was curious about was the fact that something was on Eldridge's schedule that he wasn't aware of.

Stone watched Sheen and Riley walk down the hall and disappear into Riley's office. Jensen then knocked on the door to the small office located next to the Governor's, the office that belonged to Jonah Fisk.

Fisk looked up, saw Stone and greeted him, "Afternoon, sir."

"Who was the Governor just meeting with?" Stone asked, choosing the direct approach as the best one.

"I... perhaps you had better talk to the Governor about that, Mr. Stone," Fisk replied, not wanting to betray his boss's trust. That was, after all, the key component to their relationship and Fisk couldn't properly do his job without it.

"Boy, you two are just thick as thieves these days, aren't you? All kinds of secrets that the rest of us have to learn about after the fact."

Fisk didn't respond but his expression showed the discomfort he felt being in this rock and a hard place position.

"Is he alone now?" Stone asked.

"Yes, sir."

Stone entered the Governor's office. Before attempting any pleasantries, Stone started right in on Eldridge.

"Let me tell you how things get fouled up and how we no longer function as successfully as we have for the last three years. When I don't know things, when I'm finding my position of chief of staff is a position that is frequently uninformed, then I can't run your administration from a day-to-day standpoint."

Eldridge stared at Stone, irritated with the way he simply waltzed in and began to gripe. So there was no shortage of sarcasm when the Governor asked, "Something on your mind, Jensen?"

"Who are you meeting with and why don't I know about it?"

"I do that sometimes. Yes. Offensive though it may be to your sensitive self image, I sometimes have meetings that you're not aware of. From time to time I just want information without your political counsel."

"Well, that's a very dangerous road, sir."

"Well, that's tough. And I'm assuming you're talking about that gentleman who was just in here. He's a private detective, he's from Miami and he's been looking into Etta's murder."

"God damn it!"

Eldridge stood up, pointed at Stone, but did not get in his face. He let his words do that. "This is why I didn't tell you about this meeting, because you would not have let me see him."

"No kidding!"

"But I need to know what happened to her, and it doesn't have anything to do with me and it doesn't have anything to do with the election. But you just have too much of a one-track mind to acknowledge that."

Stone sighed, took a seat and thought the matter over. Eldridge took his seat behind the desk, then finally asked, "What?"

Stone calmly explained, "I understand your need to find her killer, I'm not insensitive to that. But what is sensitive is the truth about the Governor of a southern state having had a romance with a Negro woman. I don't know this detective, I don't know what he's about. What guarantees do we have that he won't let that be known?"

"I believe he's discreet. Just talking to him here, I don't think he's going to say anything about it."

"I love you for your compassion, you know that. You're too trusting, my friend. Far too trusting."

↟ ↟ ↟

After Sheen's meeting with the Governor, Riley asked Ben if he'd like to get some dinner later and discuss the Etta Childs case. Sheen agreed and he joined Riley at a burger joint on Monroe Street, just north of the Capitol Building.

As Sheen chewed on his medium rare burger with mushrooms and swiss, Riley talked about his experience working for the

Governor. He seemed to like what he was doing, feeling like he was part of something that mattered. Though he did miss being a newsman, ultimately he felt his move had been worth it.

Then they began to talk about Etta. Sheen clued Riley in on the progress he'd made and people he'd talked to. The Detective enjoyed putting the information in front of fresh eyes. He didn't sense any danger from Riley and thought the mind of a former investigative journalist might help point out a few things, bring up new questions. Anything would be welcome, especially considering that Sheen was beginning to feel his trip to Tallahassee was turning into a waste of time. All he figured that he'd accomplished was crossing the name of Nathaniel Eldridge off the list of possible suspects. And that list was nearly non-existent. The only new information he'd picked up in his conversation with the Governor was about the producer on Etta's last picture. And even though he would look into it, Sheen's instincts were the same as Eldridge's in the matter. He felt it would amount to nothing much at all.

"Listen," Sheen told Riley. "I need you to keep this thing about Etta and the Governor under your hat until I can get to the bottom of things."

Riley waved him off with a gesture, not needing to be reminded. "I have no intentions of talking about that to anyone. Something like that, politically... he'd be finished. I have no reason to take him down. Besides, I'm not a newsman anymore."

Sheen nodded, then tentatively approached the subject. "You know, Riley... Given the fact that this could ruin a man, and the fact that you were really the only one writing about her murder... Don't you think it's strange that you get a call, clear out of the blue, to stop reporting and go work for the administration of a man whose secret affair with a Negro actress may have been uncovered had you kept digging?"

The thought hadn't crossed Riley's mind. But now it was all he could think about. The two sat in silence as Riley finished off his french fries and Sheen sipped on his coke with cherry flavoring from the soda fountain.

CHAPTER 15

UNDER WATCHFUL EYES

Josh Riley sat in his office, going over a new draft for a speech the Governor was to give to the Florida Citrus Commission when Jensen Stone stepped in. He closed the door behind him just as soon as he walked in the room.

Riley looked up, eyes raised in curiosity and asked, "What do you need, Mr. Stone?"

"I know what you did last night," Stone said. "Going to dinner with that Detective. What's he snooping for?"

Riley shrugged then responded, "He was updating me on the murder of an actress in Miami. I'd written a couple stories about it, the murder was never solved. He'd reached out to me about a month ago and he was just giving me the latest."

"A private detective from Miami travels all the way up here to give you progress on the murder of a colored actress, I don't think so."

Riley stayed quiet for a moment, then added, "I never said she was colored, sir."

Stone grimaced and bit the inside of his lip, realizing he let something slip there. Nevertheless he kept a firm stare affixed on Riley.

"He told me about a few people he'd talk to, suspects he'd ruled out. That's all." Riley tried to hold his poker face, not sure if Stone was in on the tip that Eldridge had been dating Etta.

Stone, on the other hand, didn't believe that Riley hadn't been given that information by Sheen. "I think you know more than that. And I know that he met with the Governor yesterday," Stone said.

"Okay."

"And I'm probably also right in guessing that you arranged that meeting."

Riley didn't respond, knowing he may have been out of professional bounds in doing so, but felt the murder of a woman was more important than protocol.

"Listen to me... You don't speak to him again. The Governor does not speak to him again. Stay away from that detective, let me take care of him and you don't get involved in things that are outside of your purview."

Riley felt the threat, subtle though it was. His instincts told him that his job was in danger, but that Detective Sheen was possibly in a greater form of danger. He simply, dutifully responded to Stone's words by saying, "Yes, sir."

Stone kept his authoritative glance on Riley for another moment before he opened the door and exited.

⅄ ⅄ ⅄

Sheen sat at his dining table across from Mickey. Both enjoyed a cigarette. Sheen shook his head and admitted to Mickey, "I fear that my trip was basically a waste of time."

"Why didn't you just call?" Mickey asked. "Seems like a lot of trouble to go all the way out there for a couple of conversations."

"You're a card player, Mick. You can't read faces over the phone."

"That's true enough. So what about this producer fellow? You think he's got something to do with it?"

"No. I'll talk to him anyway, but honestly..."

Sheen's thought was interrupted by the ringing of his telephone. Sheen stood up to answer it. As he walked to the phone he finished his thought, "I think it's a pretty weak motive."

Sheen answered the phone, "Hello."

The voice on the other end of the line was Josh Riley's. He told Sheen about his meeting with Stone and warned Sheen that he should keep his eyes open. He also announced to Sheen that he had turned in his resignation. He was completely convinced, at this point, that the only reason he had been hired in the first place was to get him away from the Miami News desk and off the story of Etta's murder. He left Sheen with a home telephone number where he could be reached and wished the detective luck.

$$\lambda \quad \lambda \quad \lambda$$

Later that evening, Sheen was driving his Coupe north on Northwest 7th Avenue. He turned right on 10th street and was heading towards Serena's apartment. They'd made a date to have dinner together. After several blocks, Sheen had noticed that an Olympic Blue Buick Roadmaster was keeping its distance behind him, trying not to be seen following the detective.

Before jumping to conclusions and being paranoid, Sheen decided to test his theory by going on a bit of a joyride. When Sheen got to Northeast 1st avenue, he turned right. He drove south for a while, seeing that the Buick was still in his rearview mirror. When he came to the courthouse on 1st street, he made a left and drove east, towards Biscayne Boulevard.

The Buick was still behind him and Sheen couldn't help but wonder if the car had recently had new rear tires installed. Which is to say, could this be the same Buick Roadmaster that Sheen saw parked outside of The Gin Mill a few weeks back, that belonged to Lt. Granville of the Miami police department?

Sheen pulled over to the curb and got out of his car. He looked out of the corner of his eye to see that the Buick had stopped at the far end of the block. That clearly indicated to Sheen that he was being followed. He reached into his pocket and pulled out some coins. He stepped up to a pay phone on the corner of Northeast 2nd avenue and dialed Serena's number.

The sweet sound of her voice gave Sheen a grin as she answered, "Hello."

"Hello, darling," Sheen replied. "I've got some bad news. I can't see you tonight."

Serena's voice gave way to disappointment, but the tone of concern was more evident. "Is everything all right?"

"Everything's fine." Sheen didn't see the sense in worrying her. "How's about we have lunch tomorrow. Maybe we'll go to Friendly's? Nobody seems to bother us there."

"Okay, I'd like that."

"Terrific. I'll call you tomorrow."

"I love you."

"I love you too, sweetheart."

That was the first time they had shared those words with each other. There was nothing dramatic about it, not even a moment's contemplation. Both said it as simply as if they'd been used to saying it for years. Sheen thought on that for a moment and wondered if Serena was as well. He wasn't scared by it, he wasn't put off at all. More than anything, he was amused at how comfortably it had been exchanged.

"Good night, Serena."

"Good night."

Sheen hung up the phone and walked towards his car. As he walked around the front of the vehicle, keeping his head bowed so the brim of his fedora might hide his stare, he raised his eyes to identify the Buick waiting in the distance.

Sheen got in the Coupe and drove down second, turning right on Flagler, driving past the Olympia Theater and finally doubled back around to the courthouse on 1st. He parked his car across the street at the Nickel Dime coffee shop, subtly acknowledging the Buick that had crept around the corner as he entered the diner.

Sheen took a seat facing the front door. His usual waitress, Doris wasn't there. She worked the morning and early afternoon shift. The only person in the shop that Sheen knew was a busboy named Eugene, a wiry kid of nineteen, sort of intellectual and was usually very talkative about basketball. Eugene thought that Bob Cousy of the Boston Celtics was the greatest man alive and Eugene was convinced that Cousy and Bill Sharman could lead the Celtics to a championship. Sheen didn't know much about the game, but knew that George Mikan and the Minneapolis Lakers had been the team to beat the past few years. Still he didn't find the game as interesting as baseball and wasn't convinced that the three year old National Basketball Association could ever compete with the national pastime.

Sheen sipped at a cup of coffee, lit up a Camel and waited. In fact he'd sat there nearly forty-five minutes before he asked Eugene to step outside and see if the Buick was still waiting.

After a few moments, Eugene returned with the news that the car was in fact parked on the curb up the street. Sheen asked Eugene to do him a favor and gave the busboy some instructions.

Lt. Granville sat in his Buick Roadmaster, keeping an eye on the coffee shop that was just down the street from where he knew Detective Sheen's office to be. When he first saw Eugene walking towards his car, he didn't think much of it. That was until Eugene walked right up to the driver's side door and gently knocked on the window.

Granville rolled down the window and furrowed his brow, giving the kid his best cop stare.

"Detective Sheen says why don't you come in, he'll buy you a cup of coffee," Eugene nervously said.

Granville's face went flush with embarrassment. Then he nodded his head and closed his window. He got out of the car and followed the busboy into the coffee shop. He shook his head and flashed a frustrated grin at Sheen. Then he pulled up a seat across from the private detective and sat down.

"Hell of a night, isn't it?" asked Sheen. "Still, hot."

Granville shrugged. "It's not so bad," the overgrown weasel responded.

"Coffee's fresh, they just put it on a couple of minutes ago. Care for a cup?"

"Sure."

Sheen nodded to his waitress and asked for a cup of coffee for Lt. Granville. The cop studied the private eye, wondering what he'd brought him into this coffee shop for and what he wanted.

"How's everything in that big building over there?" Sheen asked.

"What do you want, Sheen?" Granville questioned.

"You're the one following me, Granville. Why don't we start with that?"

"I'm keeping an eye on you."

"Why?"

"You're working a case that is currently an open murder investigation by the police department."

"A murder that you fellas didn't give a damn about a month ago, so what else is going on?"

"You trying to tell me how to run my squad?"

"Let's not make this a pissing contest, Lieutenant. It'll put me off my coffee cake."

"You know more than you should, simple as that. A two-bit private detective like you that couldn't cut it as real police can't know the things you know. I'd like to know how."

"I'd like to know how *you've* got the inside dope on what I've been able to uncover. Just exactly who are you in bed with, Granville?"

Granville chuckled, reached into his pocket and pulled out a pack of Chesterfields. He struck a match and lit up the cigarette he'd just taken from the pack. He let out the smoke from his first drag and said, "I'm protecting people's interests, who they are isn't really your business."

Then a sly smile crept across Granville's face. Sheen saw Granville's bushy eyebrows raise with the expression and he thought the lieutenant almost looked like a wolf. Even the smile had a beastly quality, one of the pack ready to pounce and enjoy the kill.

"You know something, Lieutenant," Sheen stated. "You remind me of the scorpion and the frog."

"How's that?"

"A scorpion and a frog meet at the bank of a stream. The scorpion wants to cross to the other side so he asks the frog to carry him across on his back. The frog asks 'How do I know you won't sting me?' And the scorpion tells him 'If I did, then both of us would die'. So the frog agrees, lets the scorpion crawl onto his back and they set across the stream. But midstream the scorpion stings the frog. The frog starts to lose all feeling to paralysis and both of them begin to sink, soon to drown to their deaths. The frog asks 'Why would you do this? It's completely illogical?' And the scorpion replies 'I can't help it. It's my nature'."

Granville took another puff off his Chesterfield and asked, "Meaning what?"

"You're a shitheel no matter who you're working for, Granville."

Granville's expression went as solid as stone as he stared down Sheen. And Sheen refused to give him the satisfaction of backing down, he returned the look with a solid stare of his own.

"You sure you really want to test me, Sheen?"

"Look, how long are you going to be tailing me?"

"Why are you so hell bent on this thing? Tell that uppity nigger you couldn't find anything on his sister's killing, collect your money and move on."

"He's my client. I'm hired to do a job, I do it until the trail runs cold. And this one's not cooled down."

"You're looking into a whole lot of nothing and when it all comes down to it the only ones who are going to give a damn about that actress are her people and a few friends."

"I think I'm done with my coffee."

Sheen stood up and walked towards the front door. He was stopped by Granville's hand on his arm.

"Don't be a fool, Detective."

Sheen pulled a Camel out of his pocket, lit it up and brushed away Granville's arm with just enough force to stand his ground, but not enough to really anger the Lieutenant.

"You can't follow me twenty-four hours a day, Lieutenant. You may not do it worth a damn, but I believe you still have a day job to go to."

Sheen stepped up to the door and opened it.

"Go to hell," Granville said.

Sheen said over his shoulder, as he walked out, "Not as long as you're there, pal".

Sheen walked to his Coupe, got inside, started the engine and drove off into the dark, Miami night.

CHAPTER 16

PROCEED WITH CAUTION

Serena was wearing a gorgeous blue dress that complimented her figure as she walked into her brother's diner. She was a radiant woman whose recent romantic life had given her a boost in her own self image. It had nothing to do with Ben Sheen, specifically, but the status of being in love. It had been a long while since Serena had been seeing anyone and just being in a relationship, knowing she was wanted, she felt sexier to herself.

The diner had a few customers. A young man with his newspaper occupied a table in the corner and an elderly couple shared a meal at one of the other tables. A lone man, white, sat at the counter. His head was low to his plate as he gobbled up his rice and black-eyed peas with the cornbread he'd crumbled into it. Serena had almost done a double take when she saw him. It's not that white people had never eaten at Wendell's place, but it was rare enough to give one pause when they saw it.

Serena carried a bag from which she produced a covered plate and handed it to Wendell, who was in his usual spot behind the counter. "Corn fritters," she said. "Just had me a taste for them and a whole batch is more than I needed."

"Mama's recipe?" Wendell asked, his eyebrow raised and face showing a devious smile.

"Of course."

Wendell's smile grew larger and he placed the plate behind the counter.

Serena then took the summer dress she'd borrowed from Pearl a few days back and handed it to Wendell. "It's been washed. Please thank Pearl again for me," Serena requested.

Wendell took the dress and placed it behind the counter as his expression grew more serious and he stared at Serena. "We gonna talk about that other thing?" he asked.

Serena shrugged it off, assuming Wendell was referring to the truth about their sister and Florida's governor.

"Uh-uh, baby sister. Don't just toss it aside like it ain't nothin'. It is somethin'. You ever think Etta would be the kind to do somethin' like this?"

Serena didn't know how to react. The way Wendell chose his words... 'the kind to do something like this'. That troubled her. At the same time she understood his point of view.

"I don't know. It's shocking."

"Damn right it is."

"Hush up with that kind of language, there's no call for it." Serena had lowered her voice to keep the conversation private. Even though Wendell spoke in a hushed tone, his whispered voice had plenty of anger and passion to it.

"Oh, come on now, Sesa! White man takin' advantage of our sister like that? And it don't make it no better that Henrietta was damn fool enough to fall for it!"

"I don't want you talking ill of her! It's not right, she was our sister and somebody killed her."

"Murdered or not, I wish I could go back and talk some sense into that girl."

"Wendell, you mind your tongue."

Wendell noticed that the man who sat several stools down at the counter had taken a last sip of his coffee. Wendell instinctively grabbed the pot behind him. But before he walked over to the man he looked at Serena and added, "You're too kind hearted. That's your trouble."

Wendell approached the man and asked, "More coffee, sir?"

The man replied, "Yes. Thank you."

Wendell refilled the man's cup and the man added, "This is, by far, the best Hoppin' John I ever ate." The man finished his statement with a warm smile.

"Well, thank you, sir. I'm pleased to hear that," Wendell replied. As he walked back to put the coffee pot down he thought the pleasantness of the interaction was strange. He had rarely experienced such kindness from white folks. Ben Sheen was all right, he guessed. But most of the time it was a race best steered clear of. A race that Henrietta didn't have any business mixing with in such a familiar fashion.

Again in a hushed tone, he spoke to Serena. "I ought to march on up to that building and tell that Eldgridge what's what. Give him a piece of my mind and tell him just what he can do with it."

"Don't even joke like that, Wendell," Serena exclaimed!

"Ain't no joke, Sesa! Him gettin' involved with our kin, that ain't right! Ain't natural and should somebody tell that man."

"It's too dangerous. You can't cause trouble like that with big shots like those politicians they got up there."

"Oh, but Detective Sheen can 'cause he white!"

"Just let him handle it the way he sees fit is all."

"Let me tell you something, baby sister. I don't like you spendin' the time you been spendin' with him."

"What are you talking about?" Serena asked, trying as best as she could to hide the fear that Wendell knew what was going on.

"Just don't act so friendly around him is all. I seen the way that man looks at you and I ain't havin' that. He might seem all nice and the like, but I think he's just like that fancy governor, messin' around where he ought not to be messin'!"

"Now you listen here. You may not like what went on, but before she was gone, Henrietta told me she was in love. And I never saw her as happy as I did those last months. And white or not, that man was the person our sister was in love with. So whatever you think about it being right or wrong, you need to have some respect for the love that she had."

Wendell chuckled, "That's the silliest thing I ever heard outta you." Wendell stared, as serious a look as he'd ever given, and with disgust he stated, "Love between them two people ain't possible. And if you believe different, then you a damned fool."

Serena's heart sank. Sadness filled her face and she shook her head at her brother. Without a word she stood up from the stool, turned around and walked away. Wendell saw her leave the diner.

What he didn't see was the white man sitting at the end of the counter watching him as he saw his sister walk away. The man was the kind of fellow who could get lost in the crowd. That's why he was very good at what he did. He could sit in a room with a cup of coffee and a plate full of food and appear to be minding his own business.

But the truth was that he'd heard every word of Serena and Wendell's conversation. Wendell didn't see that either.

Virginia Key was east of the Miami mainland, situated between Biscayne Bay and the Atlantic Ocean. Friday nights Mickey Wails could always be found at a stone crab restaurant on the island named The Inlet Grill, but card players commonly referred to it as "the stone crabbers joint". The restaurant had been built up twelve feet from the ground, a set of stairs leading to the entrance. The common belief was that fear of flooding during hurricane season caused the original owners to keep the restaurant well above sea level. But those in the know realized that it provided the necessary space for the poker, blackjack and roulette games that were illegally held beneath the floors of the legitimate business.

Most of the Friday night gamblers were the very men who worked all week, shucking oysters and peeling shrimp for preparation in the kitchen. And Mickey was well known among the mixture of white, black and Caribbean men who put their money on the table in pursuit of financial fortune mixed with recreation.

Sheen had needed a night of relaxation and he knew that an evening at the tables with Mickey always proved to be a gas. So he met his pal at the stone crabbers joint, feasted on crab legs, conch chowder and hush puppies, then went downstairs to play some seven card stud.

Sheen ran well for about an hour, even taking a big pot off of Mickey when his queens full of nines topped Mickey's three aces. But after a while he began to hit some cold spots and the hands just weren't there anymore. In the end, Sheen walked away with thirty bucks of profit from his winnings. It would have been sixty, but his jack-high straight fell to a flush that one of the shrimp peelers made with his last down card.

Sheen drove home, thinking that he hadn't seen Serena for a few days. He'd thought that was best, given the surveillance he believed he was under. Though he hadn't seen Granville's blue Roadmaster since the other night. And he hadn't noticed anyone else following him, something that he kept close watch on.

When he pulled into his driveway, he yawned, finally coming down from the excitement of the evening. It was late, the early morning hours, and he was ready to drop into his bed. Sheen was careful to shut the door of the Coupe as quietly as possible at this shade of night. He walked up to the front door and unlocked it.

Sheen stepped into the house and was about to turn on the light when he noticed a newspaper on the kitchen table was fluttering ever so slightly. There was a bit of wind outside but with the front door closed behind him he couldn't figure how the paper was catching any breeze. Unless the side door in the kitchen that led out to the rear corner of the property had been opened.

He moved slowly as he reached in at his holster and pulled out his Colt. He knew it couldn't be Mickey this time, he'd left him earlier at the card table. Sheen noticed, as he walked closer to the kitchen, that a light emanated from down the hall. He believed it to come from the bathroom, but chose to first conclude his investigation in the kitchen. More alarming was the blood on the floor that trailed through the living room into the kitchen and going the opposite way down the hall.

He led with the barrel of his gun first and searched the area, finding no one in the room and no immediate danger in that location. A quick inspection of the door showed no signs of forced entry, so someone may have gotten into his house another way, but they left through the back door.

His attention turned to the other room and the trail of blood. He proceeded with gun pointed at the ready. As he passed each room going towards the bathroom, he looked in each, making sure nobody was standing there, waiting for him. The trail continued down the hall, past the bathroom.

Finally he reached the bathroom door and he quickly turned on his heels, pointed the gun in the bathroom and stood at the ready. No one was there. He cautiously, in his defensive stance, pushed the shower curtain aside to find nobody in the tub. The only thing he noticed about the room was the writing on the bathroom mirror. It was written in black and the smell gave off the tell-tale aroma of shoe polish. The message read: Leave the dead nigger alone.

He stepped back into the hallway and followed the blood trail into the guest bedroom, which had years earlier been his son's room and was still decorated for a child. He clicked the switch on a lamp and the room lit up. He saw no one in the room and opened the closet door to make a final check. Though his gun was still in hand, Sheen relaxed his posture as he observed the state of the room. The first thing he'd noticed was the shattered window and the minor traces of blood that were on the sill, accompanied by a single shell casing that had been ejected from a fired weapon.

The second thing that the detective took note of was the greater amount of blood that had spilled on the floor. A small puddle near the bed and smeared blood across the greater portion of the wood floor. An additional shell casing rested on the ground.

Someone had busted in and something violent had occurred, which led Sheen to his next thought.

"Doyle? Doyle!" He called out for his bull terrier, then whistled after him. He hurried through the house, calling after the dog and searching each room with his .38 automatic at the ready.

Satisfied with the interior search, he walked out the backdoor and searched the surrounding yard. "Doyle," he called out! "Where are you, boy?" Another whistle went unanswered.

There was a tin shed on the property, behind the house, that Sheen used more as a task garage than anything else. He had some woodworking tools in there, his lawn mower and most basic necessities for automobile maintenance. Sheen retrieved a flashlight and searched the yard further.

At the outside wall, where the guest room window was located, Sheen saw some smudges of blood on the house. Then a bloody shoeprint pressed into the grass and what may have been a bloody paw print. Two more shell casings were on the ground. Sheen got increasingly nervous as he scanned the area and his voice broke a little as he called out, "Doyle! Come on, boy!"

His search continued to the other side of the house where the beam from his flashlight picked up on something in the grass. A small white item stood out and Sheen knelt down to inspect it. A cigarette butt, not quite burnt down to the printing. The brand: Chesterfield. You son of a bitch, Granville, Sheen thought.

Sheen heard a series of short but strong barks off in the distance. Sheen turned, looked and shouted "Doyle!" Then he gave a loud whistle. Sheen ran around to the front of the house, fairly certain that the bark came from that direction.

As he reached the sidewalk, Sheen peered into the darkness on the street and could barely make out some movement in the distance. He didn't point the gun out, but he kept it at his side, ready to raise at the moment's notice of danger. The blur in the darkness grew bigger and as it came closer it also came into focus.

It was Doyle, cautiously walking forward. Once Sheen recognized his pet he dropped down on one knee and called out "Come here, boy!" Sheen clapped his hands and then spread them apart.

Doyle barked and picked up the pace to a jog as he approached his master. The moment just before Doyle arrived at Sheen's arms he had a slight whimper. He was happy to see Sheen, but had been through some sort of ordeal. "Good boy," Sheen said. "It's okay, boy."

Sheen petted Doyle and looked him over. There was blood around Doyle's mouth, but no injuries around that part of his body.

The blood must have been from the intruder, whom Doyle seemed to have gnashed his teeth into. The only marks anywhere on Sheen's trusty companion were a couple of scratches on his right side. They were far from serious and Sheen was relieved.

As Sheen cleaned up Doyle's wound he thought about the event that must have occurred in his house. By the time he'd cleaned up the mess, Sheen had concluded that two men had entered. They busted his guest room window and climbed into the house, alarming Doyle. The bull terrier attacked and caught one of them with his bite, probably on the leg, causing the spillage of all that blood. Then, the other man attempted to shoot Doyle, but missed. Doyle jumped out the busted window, catching enough of a glass shard to slightly cut him. Doyle ran off and the assailant fired three more shots out the window, trying to kill the dog.

Since the blood trail never went into the bathroom, the other man must have left the message on the window and then the two of them exited through the kitchen.

Sheen stood in his dining room, lit up a cigarette and made a phone call.

"Hey, partner. I know it's very late, I'm sorry about that," Sheen said.

The voice on the other end was his former partner with the police department, Detective Tierney. "What's wrong?"

"Something's happened. I can't go into detail, but I've got big time troubles with your boss."

"What else is new?"

"No, I mean it. He's come after me and it's because of this Childress case."

"Oh Christ. That case never went anywhere, what the hell is..."

"Look, you said it yourself. The Childress murder was set aside and it had gone cold and no one gave a damn."

"That's right. They needed more manpower on the Wilby case."

"Nice story, but I think it's just a convenient excuse."

"Come on, kid. White murders get more attention, especially if it's rich white folks, you know that."

"You told me something not too long ago, about Granville. You said that he had friends with big pants. What did you mean by that?"

"Granville's been known to do some favors for politicians, upper society types, high-powered lawyers and bankers."

"Politicians up north? The state house for instance?"

Tierney sighed, "Yes. He's got connections to Tallahassee."

Sheen nodded, a grimace of irritation crept along his face and he said, "That's what I thought."

Neither men spoke for a few moments and finally Tierney asked, "What are you into, Ben?"

"You shouldn't know too much. Not just now. But before this thing is over, I'm sure I'll need your help. Can I count on you?"

"Of course, partner."

"Down any rabbit hole?"

Tierney paused, not out of disloyalty, but out of concern for what he may be walking into.

"You know I'd never intentionally do anything to harm you or your job, right?" Sheen asked.

"I do."

"But things may get rocky and I'm going to need your help."

"You've got it."

"Thanks, pal."

By the time Sheen had finished his call, the sun was starting to slowly rise. He'd forgo sleep and get some eggs and toast with a strong cup of coffee on his way to the Renuart lumber yard.

Sheen spent a good part of his day boarding up the guest room window. Once he was finished, he was exhausted. He settled for a ham and cheese sandwich and a bottle of Schlitz for his dinner. Then he made an early night of it, turning in before the sun fully set, lying in bed with his Colt .38 not far from his reach.

CHAPTER 17

HARM'S WAY

S heen had finally gotten a few solid hours of sleep, something he hadn't enjoyed for a few days. He'd turned in early, so when the phone alarmed him and woke him up at eleven thirty at night, he'd slept for a good five hours.

His jaw dropped and he closed his eyes, remorseful. But the sadness had greater weight, knowing he'd be the bearer of bad news. He listened to the speaker on the other end of the line and knew he had a conversation with them, assuring the person that he was on his way. But Sheen would have no memory of it as he was stunned and nearly in a trance when he dressed, secured his gun in its holster, left the house and got into his Coupe.

⋏ ⋏ ⋏

Serena was in the passenger seat, distraught and holding a handkerchief to her eyes. Sheen drove, silent, occasionally darting his eyes to his right, checking on the woman beside him.

A few blocks from their destination, Sheen noticed a familiar vehicle, the blue Buick Roadmaster he'd been followed by the previous week, sitting in the dark off to the side of the road. At this moment there was no such thing as coincidence in his mind, particularly since he'd suspected that Lt. Granville was responsible for the break-in at his home. He didn't make any gesture or glance towards the parked vehicle, but took a mental note of its presence.

When Sheen and Serena pulled up to the 7th Street Diner in Overtown, a couple of police cars were already parked out front. Sheen led Serena past the uniform officers, into the diner.

"Oh, God," Serena wailed! "Jesus, no!"

The site of her brother, Wendell, lying on the floor behind the counter, a pool of his own blood beneath him that had seeped from the bullet wounds in his chest, destroyed Serena. She knew he had been killed. Sheen had reported that message to her when he arrived at her apartment, just as Detective Tierney had called Sheen and told him earlier that night. But walking into the place of Wendell's death and seeing him on the ground, victim of a violent act, was more than she could have prepared herself for. Sheen comforted her as she wept.

He led her towards a chair at one of the tables against the wall, where the body would be out of her line of sight. Sheen looked at one of the uniformed policemen and asked, "Officer, would you mind getting a glass of water?"

The cop walked behind the bar, looked around and located some drinking glasses. He retrieved one, filled it with water and brought it back to the table. He handed it to Serena and she sipped from it. Sheen put his hand on her shoulder. Her tears still streamed down her face, but her panicked breathing slowed. Sheen looked over at Tierney who was making notes on a notepad. "Officer, would you mind?" Sheen asked as he gestured towards Serena.

The officer sat across from her and Sheen squeezed her arm in a warm gesture of comfort. She nodded at Ben and he stepped away, walking towards Tierney.

"What are you thinking?" asked Sheen.

"Robbery gone bad," Tierney replied.

"Really."

"Thief comes in, pulls a gun on Childress and he fought back. From there things got out of control and he ended up dead."

"Wendell wasn't the kind of man to make enemies," Sheen said. As the words escaped his lips he'd thought back on Wendell's perspective on potential enemies: 'Hell with 'em, I'll outlive 'em'. Sheen shook his head and thought: Guess you were wrong this time. Sorry, friend.

Sheen looked over the area. Wendell had been shot twice in the chest. There was also some blood on his temple. Sheen noted that a few inches from the head, several drops of blood had sprinkled onto the tiled floor. The window right next to the bar had not broken, but a large crack had formed on one edge. Tiny slivers of glass had dropped down onto the sill.

"Where's Granville?"

Tierney shook his head, "Shift commander is Lt. Bellanger tonight. All week, actually. Granville's on vacation."

"Hmmm," Sheen muttered, bemused.

"What?" asked Tierney.

"This is staged."

"Come again."

Sheen stepped towards the body and looked at the wound on Wendell's head. He touched the dead man's hair and looked around the ground between the body and the window.

"No glass in his hair, no blood on the window or around the window. Somebody wanted this to look like a struggle, but it's not. The killer came in, fired two shots, then knocks Childress on the head afterwards and shatters the window for effect. Look, you can see the blood that hit the ground when the killer struck him on the head, laying right where he is now."

Tierney looked at the spot that Sheen indicated with his finger.

"And no footprints," Sheen continued. "If these guys are struggling with each other and the killing is the result, you'd have smears of blood, probably a footprint too. The guy that did this was careful not to get himself messy. I don't know how they want you to write it, partner, but this is a staged robbery to cover up a murder."

Sheen moved in closer to Tierney, leaning in to whisper, "That call I gave you last night? Those questions about Granville? This is more of his handiwork."

Tierney's face went pale, not wanting to accept it and tried to refute it when he replied, "That's a serious accusation, Ben."

"It's right, I'm sure of it. When I asked you if I could count on you for anything? This is the road we travel. You okay?"

Tierney nodded his head in affirmation.

"Give me a couple days, will you? Granville's the puppet, I need to make sure I find his master. That's gonna finish off the Etta Childs case."

⅄ ⅄ ⅄

Sheen and Serena had gone to his house. She was lying on the sofa, never far away from a tissue or handkerchief, as the tears wouldn't dry up. She felt alone, even with Sheen there.

Ben was watching out the window. Constantly aware of everything that went on around the house. Though the knock on the door startled Serena, it actually gave Sheen comfort. He answered it and in stepped Mickey.

"Anybody out there? No tail, no familiar faces?" Sheen anxiously asked.

"Nobody," Mickey replied with simplicity. Then he turned his attention towards Serena. "My sympathies for your brother".

She couldn't vocalize a response and she sniffled back a new set of tears as she nodded her appreciation for his kindness.

"What's your play?" Mickey asked.

"I need her safe. Then I'm going after the son of a bitch that did this," Sheen responded.

Serena stood up and approached the two of them. Her face moved from sadness to anger as she gave Sheen a stern look and asked, "You know who killed Wendell?"

"I have my suspicions," Sheen frankly replied.

"Tell the police!"

"No. Not yet."

Serena pulled back with her right arm, swung it around and slapped Sheen across the face. "What is wrong with you?"

"Serena, honey. I need to keep this quiet just a little longer..."

Whack! She slapped him again.

Sheen continued in spite of it, saying, "If I don't then I can't link it back to Etta's murder and then your brother's death will be in vain and your sister's will still go unsolved."

This third slap was the hardest and Sheen's face stung from the onslaught of Serena's open hand.

"You don't get to tell me that! You have no right!"

She was about to lay another one on his cheek, but Sheen grabbed both her arms and held her back, despite the strength with which she struggled. She began to break down, crying as Sheen held her.

"The last time we spoke to each other, we argued," Serena admitted. "I was angry with him and he was disappointed in me. I pitied him and I felt sorry... God forgive me." Her tears ran down her face and wet the shoulder of Sheen's shirt.

"I'm sorry, honey. I know it's terrible," Sheen comforted. He shushed her as he ran a soothing hand against her back. "Please, give me this chance. Someone needs to speak for both their murders and I can make that happen."

Serena gazed upon him with sorrowful eyes.

"And I need to keep you safe. You have to trust me," he insisted.

She agreed, quietly nodding. "Mickey's gonna take you some-place safe. You give him your keys and he'll get some clothes and whatever you need and he'll be checking in on you," Sheen added.

Concerned, Serena asked, "What about you?"

"We need to stay away from each other until all this is over."

Serena immediately kissed him. Sheen wanted to hold the kiss forever, but knew they couldn't. He held her face in his hands and looked deep into the eyes that had mesmerized him and brought him to the place where he now found himself, an important part of her life.

"He's gonna get you out of here and..."

Serena's panic temporarily returned as she asked, "What about Pearl?"

Sheen sighed, frustrated. He really didn't think that Wendell's wife was in danger, but he didn't feel comfortable taking that chance. "Once Mickey's got you somewhere safe, you need to call her and tell her to meet him, he'll take her to you."

"How do you want to do this, Ben?" Mickey asked.

⅄ ⅄ ⅄

Sheen opened the tool shed in his backyard and reached into a corner where he grasped a wooden oar. He carried it with him towards the back of his property where the grassy hill sloped down and gave way to the waters of the Miami River.

Tied around the post of a small wooden dock that Sheen had built himself, was his Dunphy Shad wooden boat with an outboard motor. Sheen liked to take it out sometimes on the weekend and runabout the local waters. But tonight it served as his best diversion and escape vehicle for Serena.

He hugged her, kissed her cheek and helped her get in the boat. Then he passed the canoe paddle onto Mickey and instructed him, "Don't start the engine unless you're well out of range."

Mickey nodded, knowing that the sound would carry and he didn't want to hurt the covert aspects of getting Serena out of here.

"Once you've gotten far enough and you're on dry land, call a cab and take her to Georgette's Tea Room," Sheen concluded.

"No problem. And don't worry, I'll take care of the widow as well."

"Thanks, Mick."

Sheen watched them shove off and saw Mickey paddle their way down the river. Serena kept her head turned, eyes focused on Sheen. He returned her stare, locked into a loving but sad glance that lasted until the boat was too distant to identify.

Ben went back inside his house and looked for the scrap of paper on which he'd written the number where Josh Riley could be reached. He called and Riley answered, a weary and confused tone in his voice that told Sheen the call had woken him.

"I'm sorry for waking you, Mr. Riley. But this is Detective Ben Sheen in Miami and I need to speak with you. It's urgent," Sheen said.

"Not at all, Detective," Riley responded as he gathered his bearings and asked, "What's the problem?"

"There's been an incident. I prefer not to get into the details, but something's happened and I need to be blunt. Who can you put me in touch with at the State house that you trust that has detailed knowledge on who the Governor would be in contact with?"

Riley thought about it for a moment, then replied, "What are you thinking, Detective?"

"I don't know who killed Ms. Childs but we know what was going on with her and the Governor and I know that someone down here does a little work on the side for someone in the capital. So I need to talk to somebody that I can get some answers from, but it's got to be someone that will give me honest answers to the questions I have."

"Jonah Fisk. He's the Governor's main protection official. He'll know everything that's going on at that level and he's a good man. He might not be willing to give out much information on the Governor, but he'll know everything that's going on around him. I'll talk to him, I'll let him know you're just trying to run a true investigation and he can trust in your discretion."

"I appreciate that, Mr. Riley. Thank you. We'll be in touch."

"All right. Hey, I may even run into you. I handed in my resignation, I'm moving back to your neck of the woods, probably going to get back into journalism."

"Have you got some money set aside, Riley?"

"A little. Why?"

"If I were you, I'd take a vacation for a few weeks, stay out of Miami just now. I don't know if you're being followed or not, but it seems like anyone who's had any kind of connection to the Childress case is being watched. You may want to go spend some time elsewhere. Someplace that couldn't possibly have any connection to Etta Childs."

"Thanks for the tip," Riley said.

"Thanks for the help," Sheen responded.

⅄ ⅄ ⅄

Mickey and Serena sat in the back seat of a taxi, travelling towards Brownsville. The sun was coming up and Serena was despondent and Mickey could see it on her face. He looked out the window, staring off into the distance and said, "Giancarlo Lazzeri".

Serena looked up at him and asked, "I'm sorry?"

"When I was in the war, before I worked Intelligence, I had to go through basic training like everyone else. I spent most of that time with a guy from Pennsylvania named Giancarlo Lazzeri. He was a character, always had a funny story to tell. No matter what you were coping with, he could always cut you up with a good laugh. We sort of stuck together because he was a transported Italian and I was a transported Englishman and here we were, fighting for the U.S. in the second world war. He introduced me to girls back when I was too shy to chat them up... if you can believe that."

He chuckled and Serena smiled, the first smile she'd had since the day before.

Mickey continued, "And actually he introduced me to the first love of my life, if you can believe that!"

Serena's smile gave way to an actual laugh, though the sadness in her eyes wasn't going away.

"Anyway, he was an infantryman, but we were still located close enough as we made our way through France that we'd see each other on leave or any precious little down time we could enjoy in between combat. There was this small town we'd set up in and we had a building where intelligence had taken up temporary dwellings. And down the street of this... really more like a village than a town, there was a building that had been turned into an Allied Forces military hospital."

Mickey paused, furrowed his brow as the memory returned, fresh in his mind. "I was reading a map, we were trying to figure the best approach to the German soldiers camp about twenty miles north of this town. When all the sudden I heard the loudest most terrifying boom I'd ever heard. The Germans had shelled the hospital down the road. We rushed out to see how we could assist and found the building had caved in. Giancarlo Lazzeri, my old pal, was in the rubble. He'd been escorting injured soldiers from the battlefield to the hospital. They'd just arrived before the explosion happened."

Mickey's eyes glossed over with a thin veil of tears, but they didn't trickle from his eyes. Serena's face had contorted back to concern and sadness as she listened to the story.

"I remember I wanted to march into that soldier's camp and kill every last one of those Nazi sons of bitches with my own hands. But there was this army priest, Father Lonnergan. Now if you've ever seen any Hollywood picture with an Irish Catholic priest in it, you've seen Father Lonnergan."

Mickey smiled and Serena couldn't hold back her chuckle.

"He sat me down, spoke with me for probably a half an hour. Some of what he said made sense, some of it I couldn't fully agree with. But he saw my anger and he saw my sadness. There was one thing he told me that I never forgot and it's the simplest piece of advice, but it has helped me through every loss I've felt since."

Mickey turned and looked at Serena. He put his hand on hers and told her, "Don't make an enemy out of grief. It has its purpose."

Serena bit her lip and swallowed back tears. She said, "Thank you." Then she leaned over and kissed Mickey on the cheek. "You're a peculiar man, Mickey," she continued, "And I suspect you're the kind that trouble always seems to find. But you're kind and you are very sweet."

Mickey smiled, knowing that what she'd said was all true, but appreciated the compliment on the better natures of his character.

Moments later Serena and Mickey stepped into the front entrance at Georgette's Tea Room. The same pleasant woman that had been the hostess when Sheen first interviewed The Lady approached them.

"May I help you?" the hostess asked and she gave the mismatched duo a curious look.

"Do you have any rooms available just now?" Serena politely inquired.

"We do have one, how long do you care to stay?"

"I'm not sure."

"I'm sorry?"

Mickey spoke up, "Ma'am. I know this sounds strange, but this lady needs a place to stay... discreetly."

The hostess found the request very odd and responded, "I wouldn't want to get involved in anything unseemly."

"No, no. Nothing like that, it's just..." Mickey tried to figure the best way to explain.

By now several of the people sitting in the surrounding area, relaxing, enjoying breakfast or coffee, were looking, unable to avoid eavesdropping.

Serena interjected, "I'm in a bit of danger. Not trouble, at least not in the way of something I'd done wrong. But I do need someplace to stay and my sister once kept residence here for a time."

"And who is that, may I ask?"

"Etta Childs."

The hostess' eyes widened, appreciation and sorrow merged in her expression. Sitting nearby, and having overheard, The Lady stood from her table and walked over to the conversation.

"Serena?" The Lady asked as she took in Henrietta's sister with her eyes.

"Yes, Ma'am."

"I knew Etta very well. She was very dear to me."

Mickey stared at The Lady as recognition overtook his face and he asked, "Aren't you Marguerite Sloane?"

The Lady gazed at Mickey and a wide smile spread across her lips. "It's been so long since anyone has called me that."

Mickey continued, "I saw you at the Cotton Club in '33. You sang *Yesterdays*."

The Lady asked, "Did you enjoy it?"

A slight grin flashed on Mickey's face as he honestly replied, "It was so beautiful it broke my heart."

The Lady returned the smile and took in the finest true compliment she'd received for her talent in quite some time. "Thank you, young man," she offered. She turned her attention back towards Serena, put an arm around her and said, "You're safe here, sweetheart. That you can be sure of."

The hostess nodded. Mickey added, "She needs to be an unregistered guest. We can pay more for the inconvenience."

The hostess responded, "No need for that now. We take care of our people."

Serena looked at Mickey and reminded him, "Pearl?"

"Call her as soon as you can, tell her to meet me at the Monarch Diner off of second. Tell her to ask for Mr. Dee and wait for me. I'll have her here this afternoon."

Serena placed a hand on his shoulder and said, "Thank you."

Emotion took her for a moment and she closed her eyes, not wanting to make a show of it and, frankly, sick of her own tears. She opened her eyes, but her head was still lowered. Mickey took her chin between his thumb and index finger and lifted it up, keeping it steady and having her eyes meet his. He gave a quick, affirmative nod and said, "You're okay."

Mickey smiled at the other two ladies then turned around to head for the door. As he walked out he thought about how much he liked Serena and how much he liked her for Ben. And he hoped she would be safe and sound throughout this messy ordeal.

CHAPTER 18

FACE OF THE ENEMY

Jonah Fisk was used to the train ride across the state. Travel was a frequent activity in his vocation. Wherever the Governor went, Jonah went with him. And from time to time, Jonah went on his own. He thought about that as he glanced down at the folder on the seat next to him. He clutched it, pulling it closer to him, insuring that he would not leave it behind when he de-boarded.

When he'd received the call from Detective Sheen, he was both nervous and relieved. He had business with Sheen that the detective himself couldn't possibly yet be aware of. And it was a distasteful matter, the likes of which Fisk struggled with, ethically. Sheen had indicated that it was on Josh Riley's suggestion that he call Fisk. Jonah always liked Riley and thought him a good man. When he followed up with the recently resigned speech writer, he was told that Sheen could be trusted. From a man like Riley, that's all Fisk needed to hear.

Fisk met with Sheen at the detective's office on 1st street. They met after hours, not only to keep Mrs. Skeffington out of the situation, but also to keep the meeting quiet. Sheen hadn't seen a tail on him all day and in that respect he felt secure. Meeting in the office also gave him a personal sense of safety, if for no other reason than the comfort of familiar surroundings.

It was force of habit that caused Fisk to take mental note of all the building's exits, stairwells and windows as he worked his way up the five stories to Detective Sheen's private investigations office. He followed a couple of steps behind Sheen, who had met him downstairs at the main entrance to let him in the building.

Once they entered Sheen's place of business, they walked past Mrs. Skeffington's desk and empty chair and stepped into Sheen's office. Sheen sat in his usual spot behind his desk and Fisk sat across from him in the chair that Wendell Childress had sat in, months before, when he first employed Sheen.

"Thank you again for seeing me, Mr. Fisk," Sheen offered.

Jonah nodded then held his hand up to interrupt Sheen's speech. "Detective, I'm happy to help wherever I can. Which means wherever I feel comfortable. But I'm telling you straight off, Governor Eldridge trusts me and I value that trust. I consider it an honor to work for him and regardless of what you may think of him, the Governor is a good man."

"I really don't think anything of him. I like some of his ideas. I think that turnpike sounds like a good plan. But, honestly, I don't have much of a personal opinion either way about the Governor."

"You know secrets about him," Fisk responded, "that very few people know."

Sheen shifted in his seat, nodded and understood immediately what Fisk was talking about. "That's true, but I have no intention of using that against your boss. It's not my business at all and frankly I don't know that I have a real problem with it anyway."

"Oh, I'm sure you wouldn't," Fisk responded. Sheen didn't know what to make of that comment, but his curiosity was piqued. Fisk cleared his throat, nervously and his body language spelled out discomfort as he reached for the folder he'd carried with him on the train from Tallahassee. Fisk passed the folder across Sheen's desk, towards the detective.

"I think, before we go any further, you'd better take a look at these," Fisk instructed.

Sheen furrowed his brow as he glanced at the folder prior to grabbing it. He gave the same look to Jonah the moment before he opened the folder and pulled a number of photographs out. His heart sank and the fear was all over his face. The pictures were of him and Serena. Pictures of them at dinner together, walking with each other at various curbsides in Miami. One featured him holding a car door open for her and Serena smiling as she got inside. Funnily enough, Sheen thought that was a great shot of the two of them, like out of a Barbara Stanwyck romance and Serena's smile was radiant. Unfortunately he knew that the circumstances under which the photos were taken vastly overshadowed any pleasantness in the pictures.

Most of these were innocent enough, but the final few shots in the bunch could in no way be mistaken for what they were. They were obviously taken through the window at Sheen's house. And both he and Serena were naked in the pictures. In one photo Sheen's mouth was on the erect nipple of Serena's breast and another featured Sheen's penis in the grip of Serena's hand.

Sheen tossed the pictures aside, closed his eyes and sighed. When he opened his eyes, they met Fisk's. "So what's the story? Blackmail? I stop my investigation or you ruin me?" Sheen asked.

"No," Fisk simply replied. "I'm giving them to you."

Sheen was confused and his expression let Jonah know that. "What?" Ben asked.

"I was instructed to follow you, keep an eye on where you were heading in your investigation. Once I learned about you and Ms.

Childs' sister, I informed my employer. He told me to take pictures of the two of you."

"So you're honored to work for a man that would have you find my dirty laundry to protect his office?"

"It wasn't the Governor that had me watching you. It was his chief of staff. He's trying to nail you for breaking anti-miscegenation laws."

Sheen thought back on the conversation Riley had with Jensen Stone after Sheen had left the state house and now began to wonder if the Governor's chief of staff had connections to Lt. Granville. He looked at Fisk and confirmed, "Stone."

Fisk nodded his head.

"He ask you to do anything else?" Sheen pondered out loud. "For instance, killing Etta Childs' brother and my client?"

Fisk stared Sheen down and made a stern statement, "I wouldn't do that even if he'd asked me. But I believe your instincts are right. I think that murder was done under his orders."

"You know a man named Granville?" Sheen asked. "He's a Miami police lieutenant."

Fisk shrugged, the name meant nothing. "What's he look like?"

"An oversized weasel," Sheen responded with irritation. "Dark eyes, smallish and close together. Graying hair, buzzed in a flattop."

"Bit on the heavy side?" Fisk asked.

"M-hmm," Sheen confirmed with a nod.

"I've seen him before. He's met with Stone while we were in town."

"Doesn't surprise me. Two like that are cut from the same cloth."

"Yeah, well part of the reason I'm giving those pictures to you before Stone gets hold of them is that I don't want to take his orders anymore. Once I heard about Ms. Childs' brother I wondered about Mr. Stone's involvement. I'd spoken to Josh Riley and he'd told me about Stone's reaction to your meeting with the Governor. Then I thought through some other things and I happen to know that when Ms. Childs was murdered, Mr. Stone was out of town."

"Meaning he was gone from the state house?"

"Yes, sir. For five days. During that time we received news of Ms. Childs' passing. I was the only one that the Governor could talk to about it. Nobody else at that point knew he was seeing her and, like I said, Mr. Stone wasn't around."

"Just because he wasn't in Tallahassee at the time... that's a pretty big leap towards putting him at a murder scene across the state."

"He didn't like Ms. Childs. At least he didn't like her seeing the Governor. He'd wanted to put a stop to it and told me in confidence that he had to come up with some strategy to pull them apart."

"Killing someone is an extreme measure. And not everyone is capable of doing so."

"Mr. Stone is. He was with the Bureau of Investigation for sixteen years before the war broke out. Then he goes into the army and his qualifications earn him a place in the new special forces unit. He works mainly in interrogation. It's after the war that he gets into professional politics and works his way towards running a campaign for an old friend, Nathaniel Eldridge. The thing is, Mr. Stone likes to tell war stories and he also likes to cut loose at the end of a long week and throw a few back. A couple of nights drinking with him and I can tell you... he's gotten his hands bloody before."

"Why are you telling me this, Fisk?"

"It's important that I protect the Governor. I've never had a better job in my life. And I have come to like the man very much. Also, Ms. Childs was deserving of much better than to have it all end that way."

"How'd you find out about those two?"

"It was my job to ensure their privacy. At first I didn't care for her much. It wasn't anything personal, but I just didn't think a white man should be with a black lady in that way." Fisk though on that for a moment, then some sadness crawled across his face and he recalled, "A few months before Ms. Childs was killed, my Mama had died."

Sheen wondered what that had to do with anything they were discussing and it must have registered on his face because Jonah grinned and said, "I mention this because I had just gotten news of it and the Governor wanted me to drive Ms. Childs to a restaurant where he knew they could eat in a back room all alone. Anyhow, Ms. Childs saw I was in a bad way and asked if something was the matter. I told her that my Mama had passed on and she..."

Fisk choked up as he recalled the moment, "She kneeled down and placed a hand on my arm. She grabbed hold of it and squeezed it, the way friends do in church. She said 'You poor thing. I am so sorry for your loss'. And I looked up at her, into her eyes and the lady meant it... She *was* a lady, no doubt about that."

"If you're right about Stone, that still doesn't look very good for your boss. There's gonna be a stink around his administration and the tawdry details will come out. Many will start to wonder if he knew what Stone was doing or even planned it."

"He didn't. And I'm not wrong about Stone. You brace him and you'll learn the truth."

"Oh, I will? Listen, you've got a lot of guts coming down here and talking to me about all this. I give you credit for that, but what makes you think..."

Sheen stopped himself the moment he saw the look of concern on Jonah's face, and the curious glance he shone out the window. The moment Sheen turned to look behind him at the three panes of glass he heard Fisk shout "Down!"

Sheen dropped to the floor, as did Fisk. Glass shattered around him as several loud shots were fired from across the street. Initially, Sheen backed up against the wall beneath the window sill for protection. But when he looked across the room and saw Fisk lying on his back, one arm stretched out to his side, Sheen assumed the worst. He crawled on his knees and elbows, staying as close to the ground as possible, until he got around the desk and saw Fisk lying, looking straight up, but still breathing.

Sheen shifted his body around to use the desk as cover from the window. He examined Fisk and found the two shots that got him in the chest. "Son of a bitch!" exclaimed the detective.

Fisk reached for his jacket pocket and whimpered as his chest compressed to allow for the arm movement. Fisk couldn't quite reach.

Sheen asked, "What is it?" Fisk gestured with his hand towards the pocket inside his left lapel. "Something in your pocket?"

Sheen reached into the pocket even before Fisk could nod in confirmation. He pulled out a few folded pieces of paper, stapled together. He looked at them. "What's this, a bill?"

Fisk struggled as he spoke and said through labored breath, "For the Alcazar Hotel. A couple restaurant receipts too." Fisk grunted and his face scrunched up, his eyes squinting as he fought off the pain. He continued, "Look at the date on the hotel bill. He was here the night Ms. Childs..."

Fisk couldn't finish the sentence. He needed another gasp of breath to continue speaking. Then he grabbed Sheen's arm and demanded, "You talk to him!"

They weren't great last words but they were very much to the point. Sheen was sorry to see Fisk die in front of him, he seemed a decent fellow. But he didn't have time to think about it as he heard footsteps coming towards the outer office and the banging on the door.

He reached into his holster, pulled out his .38 and pointed it outwards, ready for use. He slowly opened his office door and cautiously stepped out into the main office. He kept low to the ground, running and ducking behind Mrs. Skeffington's desk where he stayed in cover.

The beating on the door grew louder and the impact on it was stronger. Finally the door was kicked in and a man stood in the frame with a .32 pump-action Remington rifle in hand. Sheen knew that surprise was the only way he could survive this attack. So, before the man at the entrance could make a decision on how to proceed into the office, Sheen moved around the corner of the desk enough to aim his gun and shoot the man three times. The assailant dropped his rifle and fell back on the floor, laying face-up on the threshold, his torso and head resting on the ground of the hallway.

Sheen looked at the gunshot victim and didn't recognize him. Though he might have if he'd been in Wendell's diner the day that the man who could easily get lost in a crowd was covertly eaves-dropping on Wendell and Serena's conversation, where Wendell had threatened to speak to the Governor about his relationship with Etta. It wasn't long after that that a staged robbery to cover a killing at the diner would prove to be Wendell's last experiences in life.

Sheen stepped over the body and headed for the hallway. He suspected there would be another gunman. The amount of shots that had been fired at his office windows indicated they couldn't all have come from one shooter with a pump-action rifle.

He kept his Colt at the ready and moved towards the stairs. As he approached he saw the shadow of a man ascending. He quickly turned and ran in the opposite direction. The man in the shadows picked up the pace and chased after Sheen.

As Sheen got near the window to the fire escape, the man behind him fired a shot. It shattered the glass above his head and Sheen lifted the bottom window, stepped out and kept his firearm pointed into the building, returning with two shots of his own.

"Sheen, you son of a bitch!"

He heard the man in pursuit call him out and he recognized the voice. *You bastard*, thought Sheen. He raced down the fire escape and dropped off the final, hanging ladder.

He got four steps away from the steel stairs on the side of the building before another shot came his way, so close he could feel the air pass his left ear, though it never made contact with his flesh.

Sheen turned on his heels, aimed up to the steps above, held his support hand beneath the butt of the gun and fired three solid shots at the man that was hunting him. Sheen hoped the shots were aimed as well as he thought, knowing he only had one more round in the pistol.

His worries subsided as he watched the man on the stairs grasp beneath his chest, lean forward on the railing and spill over the side, dropping the remaining three floors to the ground. Sheen heard a solid crunch along with the thud as the man's body met the cold asphalt.

Lt. Granville's devious eyes now seemed like dimming little beads that couldn't focus on anything as he lay on the pavement. The shot to his belly, and one in his right arm, were leaking blood on the ground. His gray hair had changed to a different hue as the crimson pool around his head thickened where it had smacked the street beneath him.

Sheen stood over him, a look of disdain as he watched Granville accept his fate. "Jensen Stone sent you didn't he? And he sent you after Childress too. It was you and your pal up there that killed Wendell at his diner."

Even to the last minute Granville was a true jackass, a sly grin on his face, refusing to give Sheen the satisfaction of the truth. But Sheen didn't need the confession. He knew Granville was in the area the night of Wendell's murder and knew that it had been staged by someone who knew how to invent a murder scene. And tonight he'd confirmed that Stone and Granville knew each other. It was more than enough to build a solid theory on and Stone would have to answer the questions one way or another.

Still, maybe it was the fact that Sheen never liked Granville that caused him to place the toe of his shoe on top of the open wound on his arm and step down.

The smile left Granville's face and was replaced with a scowl, powered by anguish. "Answer me, you piece of trash," Sheen commanded.

Granville attempted to spit up at Sheen's face, but lying on his back with a bullet in his gut and a dry mouth, the small amount of spittle he was able to manufacture barely popped out of his lips before it landed on the side of his own mouth and cascaded down his cheek.

Less than a minute later the stench of Granville's vacated bowels left a fitting reminder of what Sheen thought of the now former police lieutenant.

Sheen walked the block and a half to the nearest pay phone, popped a dime in the slot and called up Detective Tierney. When Tierney answered Sheen responded, "Hey partner. It's me. I hate to do this to you right now but you need to get down to my office. Something's happened."

CHAPTER 19

THE MURDER OF ETTA CHILDS

Jensen Stone sat by himself at a table next to a window in the dining car of the "Sunchaser" passenger train. He sipped from a glass that contained two fingers worth of whiskey and one ice cube, topped with soda water. It was a cool February evening and Stone was only about a half an hour out from his destination in Miami, Florida.

His mind reeled, thinking about everything he had on his desk in his Tallahassee office and the things that would never be on his desk, but that he knew he had to settle. He was proud to be a man that could handle all this business and could prepare the Governor for the work he needed to do on a daily basis, running the state's government.

He was a little uneasy as he travelled, more bothered than nervous or uncomfortable. He knew what he had to say and how to say it, but wasn't so confident that his request would be honored.

Stone didn't waste much time after he stepped off the train. He'd had his hotel reservations all settled up and decided to merely drop off his luggage then get a taxi cab to travel to Brownsville. He had the cab driver drop him off on Northwest 52nd street, at the corner of 30th court. Then he watched the taxi drive away and he walked east for several blocks until he turned onto the street where Etta Childs lived when she was in town.

He walked up to the front door and knocked, looking around at the neighborhood and seeing nobody out on the street or in their front yards. When the door opened a beautiful yet confused woman stood on the other side. Etta Childs, double-checking that her flower patterned robe was cinched tight, gave Jensen a curious stare as she said, "Mr. Stone? What are you doing here?"

Stone smiled, trying to disarm and not worry her. "I need to talk to you. It's about the Governor."

Her eyes were alarmed and the worst fears flashed in her mind. She braced herself, clutching onto the doorjamb and asked, "Is he okay? Has something happened?"

Stone held up his hand, placing the other hand on her arm and reassured her. "Oh, no. No, he's fine. Nothing's the matter with him. But I do need to speak with you."

She sighed in relief, placed her hand to her chest and breathed a little easier. "Would you like to come in?"

Stone nodded and thanked her. She let him in the door and he shut it behind him. Then she led him towards the kitchen asking, "Can I fix you a cup of coffee?"

"That would be great," he replied. "Thank you."

He sat at a small table for two that stood against a wall and held only a telephone and a silver napkin holder. Etta put the percolator on the stove, turned the knob and waited for the gas on the range to ignite the flame. Once it was lit, she adjusted the level and turned her attention towards her guest.

"What do you need to talk to me about?" she asked with a gentle politeness that was one of the appealing parts of her character.

"The governor will be running for re-election at the end of the year..." Stone wanted to let that thought sink into Etta's mind before he continued. She smiled, misreading the direction of this conversation and offered up, "Yes. I've already discussed with him the possibilities of campaigning for him in some of the districts where I might be most useful."

That was far from what Stone was thinking and, at the moment, put the exclamation point on the problem that he had to solve.

"As much as I appreciate that," he intervened, "that's not what I'm here to talk about."

"What, then?" she asked.

"This isn't easy for me to say... in some ways it isn't my business and in others, it's nothing *but* my business. And I feel for him and you, honestly... I've known him for twenty years, I knew his late wife... I've never seen him this smitten, this head over heels for anyone."

A sweet smile crept across Etta's face, even though she was wary of where this conversation was headed, she couldn't help but be pleased that Nate's feelings for her were so strong that someone else acknowledged their power.

Stone didn't notice the smile and if he had it wouldn't have made a difference. He had this point to make and it wasn't to be swayed by anything. Stone continued, "He could be President of this country. He could do so many things. When these jokers like McCarthy are gone, this nation will have to get back to battling against the *real* communist threat and Nathaniel can be the leader they'll need. He has brilliant ideas on education. He has very forward thinking on race in this country, obviously."

Stone gestured towards Etta as he made his last point. It was a wave of the hand that was almost dismissive and the remark struck Etta as slightly sarcastic. Furthermore, she didn't appreciate her relationship being likened to a social and political struggle.

"What is it you're saying, Mr. Stone?" Etta asked in very direct terms, not having much patience for this discussion.

"You need to walk away from him." It was straight to the point and Stone stared down his nose at her, his eyes locked in an authoritative glare. He knew no other way than to put it to her straightforward and with some weight behind it.

Etta pursed her lips, uncomfortable with the conversation and angry with its content.

Stone added, "President of the United States can't have a Negro girlfriend even if it's behind closed doors. The Governor of Florida shouldn't have one either. I've tried everything I can think of, but he will not listen and I'm left with only one alternative and that is to beg you to stop."

Etta stood proud as she stared him down and said, "Even if you got down on your knees..." She simply shook her head, giving him her answer. She turned away towards the coffee pot. The brown liquid was beginning to rise and bubble in the tiny glass nub on the top of the percolator.

Jensen grimaced, his eyes sad with disappointment and he reached into his pocket and retrieved a handkerchief. His brow had tiny beads of sweat that had formed. He wiped them off and tried once more, urging, "Please listen to me. This will destroy him and it won't do you many favors either. You've got to be the one to end it. He never will."

Etta's eyes smiled, though her mouth could not, given the resentment she felt towards Stone. She simply agreed, "I know he won't".

Stone stared at the back of her head as she took two coffee cups out of the cupboard. He reached into another pocket and pulled two gloves out, placing a hand in each one as he stood. He moved towards her, his stare cold and his expression empty. He had felt worse during the conversation than he did at this moment. That was a difficult discussion to have, but this felt like a necessary means to an end and he did not think on it too much.

He grabbed her quickly, immediately placing his handkerchief over her mouth to silence her. His other hand he wrapped around her throat and squeezed. She tried to fight him off, but she was no match for his strength and the best she could manage was to bruise his arm and tear the sleeve from his sport coat. Her legs went out from under her as she tried to move away. Her heels slid back and forth on the floor, looking for traction that never came. As she dropped to the ground Stone went with her.

He was convinced that she could no longer scream even if she tried so he moved his one hand to assist the other in strangling her around the throat. Tears trickled from Etta's eyes and the blood rushed to her head. She couldn't bear to look at his strained face as he choked the life out of her, so she shifted her eyes to her periphery.

She saw a few specks of dirt, perhaps miniscule bits of food, and a dust bunny on the floor beside her. And then she saw nothing, blackness shading over her view of a living world.

Stone made sure she was gone before he let go. He stood up, reached for the knob on the stove and turned off the flame beneath the coffee pot. He picked up the handkerchief that had dropped to the side of her face and pocketed it. He walked out of the room, towards the front door and exited the house.

Henrietta Childress no longer looked like herself. The eyes that had always been so full of life were now bland, unmoving and empty like a doll's eyes. Her cheeks were puffy and her beautiful brown skin had turned to an off-putting shade of gray.

At 33 years old, Etta Childs, star of stage and screen, was dead.

CHAPTER 20

PRELUDE TO PENANCE

The air was cool and smelled fresh, just after a rain storm that had lasted for nearly an hour and had left a collection of puddles scattered about the city's streets and sidewalks. Sheen sat in the driver's seat of his Coupe, wearing his raincoat. Mickey was in the passenger seat, also in a raincoat, though he called his a Mac, remaining loyal to the British colloquial.

It had been two days since Sheen had shot Lt. Granville and his goon in self-defense. Two days since he'd called his old partner Tierney to make sure the investigation was done properly, ensuring Sheen wouldn't get jammed up on some false charges. The story made sense, everything Sheen said in his statement seemed to mesh with the findings at the scene of the crime. The police captain was with Tierney every step of the way and agreed with his assessment, as well as Sheen's recollection of the incident. He did, however, for political reasons choose to keep the alleged corruption and murderous intent of why Granville was involved quiet until the time was right.

First thing Sheen did the following morning was to call the office of the Governor's Chief of Staff, Jensen Stone at the state house in Tallahassee. He had informed Mr. Stone that he would want to travel south to Miami and meet the detective at the house of the late Ms. Childs. Though Stone tried to protest and deny any need to go, as well as any connection to her unfortunate passing, Sheen insisted by telling Stone he could either face the music or read about the allegations in the Sunday paper. Stone relented and said he'd be on the next available train.

"We should have gotten some coffee. Brought a thermos, you know," Mickey stated.

"M-hmmm," Sheen replied, not really thinking about the conversation.

"We may be here a while, it's dreary out. Might have been nice," Mickey continued.

Sheen nodded slowly, his eyes focused on the street ahead of them.

The two sat in silence for a few moments, eventually broken by Mickey mentioning, "You know that Clete Tompkins kid? The boxer we questioned about Etta? I saw something in the papers the other day that he won another fight. A ten rounder against... what's his name... Burkholder. Big, meaty son of a gun. Knocked him out forty seconds into the tenth."

"Hmm." Again, Sheen was distracted and couldn't muster much of a response to Mickey's chatter. Mickey looked over at Sheen, noticing his disposition and wondered what was on his mind. Mickey knew they were waiting on a man for a rather important meeting. But he knew his pal better than that and suspected that wasn't the true reason for Sheen's disconnected manner.

Mickey decided he'd try to get Sheen's attention by having some fun with him, even if it only proved to be a sociological experiment to figure how long Ben would go before he finally heard something that caught his attention. Mickey rambled on, "I have been thinking a lot about the Communist party and, I don't know... It's not so bad.

I think I might join. It'll give me a chance to wear red more, which I don't often have the opportunity to do so. Plus the hours seem like they'd be flexible, attend a meeting from time to time..." Mickey waited, but nothing from Sheen.

He continued, "Plus I think there's an abundance of marijuana, wouldn't you guess? You think perhaps the marijuana is free? Handed to you with your first copy of Marx and a bottle of vodka?" Still nothing from Sheen. "Of course all the marijuana and the communism might hurt my chances of re-enlisting," Mickey furthered his attempts to catch Sheen's attention. "Oh didn't I tell you I'm going back into the service? Oh, sure. I've got it all planned out, you see. I get back into the military, it affords me inexpensive travel opportunities, and then I go AWOL and go into business for myself running a Filipino prostitution ring."

That finally got a reaction from Sheen as he registered the closing sentence of Mickey's pitch in his mind, looked over at his fellow veteran and asked, "What?"

"Good, so you can still hear the sound of my voice. Good to know that."

Sheen sighed, rubbed the bridge of his nose with his forefinger and thumb and responded, "I'm sorry, Mick. I'm just in my head tonight."

"What's the problem?"

Sheen shrugged it off and tried to make it seem unimportant. "This car's heavy tonight because you've got the weight of the world on your shoulders," Mickey added. "I mean, if you can't tell me..." Mickey let the thought linger, but Sheen knew the end of that sentence. Not only did he know it, he understood it and agreed with his old friend.

"I can't help but think that I got Wendell Childress killed," Sheen confided.

"Ah, come on now," Mickey said and waved it off with his hand.

"No, no, now listen to me," Sheen explained his thinking. "Why now? All this time since the murder of Etta Childs, all this time since he's been asking questions of the police. Why, suddenly, is he murdered? I don't know what he might have done or said, but a few days, maybe a week after I tell him about his sister and the governor... why after that is he killed?"

Mickey looked at Sheen and could see in his face that this really bothered him. "I don't have any answers for you, pal." Mickey continued, "But I do know this... Giving information on a case to the person that hired you, that's what you do. That's part of your job, Ben. You were hired to investigate Etta's murder, that was information that you'd gathered. If it were any other client, you'd have told them."

Sheen thought on that, nodded in agreement and accepted that Mickey's opinion was correct. Though it didn't do much to ease Sheen's feelings of guilt, and especially the sorrow over what had happened.

Sheen turned his attention back towards the road before them and the house up the block. Mickey asked, "So before all this happened, with her brother and everything, how were things between you and Serena?"

Sheen replied, "Mind your own business."

"Said the private investigator," Mickey quickly retorted.

Sheen gave Mickey a sideways glance and a halfway grin, not completely humorless at this moment. But he turned his attention forward and said, "Hey."

Sheen pointed his chin towards the street in front of them. Mickey's eyes followed and they watched as a pair of headlights grew closer. As they approached and turned into the driveway of Etta's home, the vehicle came into full view, such as it could in the darkness of the night sky. When the driver's side door opened and a man stepped out, Sheen identified him as Jensen Stone.

"That's the guy?" asked Mickey. Sheen responded with a simple nod of the head. "From what you've told me," Mickey continued, "We ought to be careful. Man like that wouldn't show up to a thing like this without some watchful eyes nearby."

"Don't worry about it, Mick," Sheen said as he opened the door of the Coupe. "It's all been taken care of."

Sheen got out of the car and was soon followed by Mickey. They walked up behind Stone as he approached Etta's front door and he turned just in time to see Sheen as the detective said, "How you doing, pal? Glad to see you accepted the invitation."

Mickey stood his ground strong behind Sheen. Stone sized up both men and Sheen nodded towards Etta's house and said, "Inside." Stone complied and moved towards the house, Sheen opening the door for him and Mickey standing close at Stone's back, ready for any sudden movement. The three men entered the home.

Sheen walked through the living room without stopping and pointed at the kitchen. "I think there's a couple of chairs in here, we could take a seat and chat," Sheen said.

Stone smiled as he followed the detective into the next room, where he had a seat at the table by the phone on the wall. "You gentlemen surely have a peculiar sense of drama about you," Stone offered.

"Why is that?" asked Sheen.

"Being here, in this place... seems sort of maudlin, wouldn't you say?"

Sheen shot a knowing look towards Mickey who shrugged as he grinned.

"You think I can't read a paper?" Stone continued, "I know this is Childs' house, I know she was strangled in the kitchen. So, what is it you're trying to prove here?"

"You were in town that night," Sheen pointed out.

"I'm often in town. Miami is a growing city, one of the fastest growing in the state, matter of fact. I'm down here all the time, part of the job."

"I'm sure," Sheen conceded. "But we have it on good authority that you weren't at all happy about the Governor's relationship and you voiced that opinion a number of times to a number of people. Some of these people being mutual acquaintances of ours... or were." Sheen let the last comment alluding to Jonah Fisk's death linger.

However, Stone didn't elaborate on it and practically ignored it when he spoke to Sheen's previous remark and said, "If you were to bother everyone that might take issue with Governor Eldridge dating a Negro, you'd never solve her murder. There would be too many suspects."

Sheen thought that Stone was not only being glib, but that he was just naturally an all-around cocky son of a bitch. But Sheen didn't let that throw him off subject and retaliated by saying, "Fair enough, but not all those people were chummy with former Lieutenant Mortimer Granville. Former meaning deader than hell."

If Sheen's making light of Granville's passing bothered Stone, it didn't show. He kept his poker face on and asked, "Lieutenant Granville?"

"Oh sure, you know Granville. Hefty fellow, no business being a police officer, let alone a Lieutenant in charge of a squad room of men."

Stone kept the act going, raising his eyes, focusing on nothing in particular, but rather feigning recollection. "Granville," he pondered. "I think I've met him once or twice when we were in town on administrative business. Big guy, yeah... gray head of hair?"

Sheen nodded and offered a further description, "Yeah. Devious head of a raccoon, sort of on the body of a manatee."

Stone's poker face flinched a bit and he was blunt when he asserted, "You certainly don't mind speaking ill of the dead, do you?"

"Depends who's dead," Sheen returned. "Look, Stone... I'm sure you've done very well in politics because there's no end to your stream of bullshit. But you knew Granville very well indeed, you've had him working this Etta Childs situation all along and I'm sure that Wendell Childress and Jonah Fisk are dead on account of you telling that son of a bitch to pull his trigger."

"You weave a wonderful tale, Mr. Sheen."

"That's *Detective* Sheen."

"Go shit in your hat. You got an official badge I don't know about? No, you don't! You left policing to the real cops so you could go take the cases of any low life that thinks they got a raw deal, including uppity coloreds that ought to have known better ways to keep their noses clean. So until you've got some actual authority, you can take your detective title and blow it out your ass!"

Sheen grinned, amused by the fight in his adversary. Mickey half shook his head, less entertained and spoke up for the first time. "This one's a real charmer, isn't he? Wonder if his bark is louder than our bite."

Stone shot a glare in Mickey's direction and asked of Sheen, "Who's this? Jerry Lewis? You boys should take this little act on the road."

"That's right," Sheen said. "We're here to entertain, put smiles on the faces of miserable cusses like you. So, yeah, he's Jerry Lewis and I'm Dean Martin."

Mickey shrugged, raised his eyes slightly with a grimace and quietly protested, "Actually, I think I'd probably be Dean Martin."

Sheen heard the comment, pursed his lips for a moment, but didn't shift his focus from Stone.

"Okay, then. You two figure it out and let me know," Stone said then attempted to walk out of the room. Before he was able to get two steps on the ground, Sheen put his hand on Jensen's chest and gently pushed him back towards the table. Mickey also shifted his weight on his heels, blocking the kitchen's entrance.

"God damn it," Stone exclaimed! "I don't know what you want me to know, let me out of here!"

"Enough of your horseshit, Stone," Sheen responded. "You're gonna stay here until you tell us about you and Granville..."

"I don't know Granville, you dumb bastard," Stone interrupted.

Sheen came right back at him, "Don't waste your breath! I know you knew the man. His last words were used to curse you for getting him into this mess and he said you should rot in hell!" Sheen lied about that part and knew that Stone had the intelligence background to see through the lie, but Sheen hoped his poker bluff would at least carry him into an admission that Granville knew Stone.

Stone studied Sheen, then he looked over the detective's shoulder to see the man's cohort, for whom Stone was a stranger. He didn't like his chances trying to get past these two and thought he'd needed another way to buy some time, keep them talking and make his escape.

He hadn't sat back down in the chair, but put his hands in his pockets and leaned against the table. "All right, Sheen. I knew Granville. Big deal. So what does that tell you, that we were in collaboration? That either of us had anything to do with this woman's death? See, *detective*, if you were a legitimate investigator and not some two-bit, back alley scrubber, you'd need actual evidential proof. Not a bunch of guess work and hearsay."

Stone slowly paced in the kitchen, making his way over towards the window where he placed two fingers in between a pair of blinds and peeked out.

Sheen reached into his jacket, stepped closer to Stone and ordered, "Get away from that window!" Sheen grabbed at Stone's arm and pulled him away.

"Relax," Stone said with the melodic tone of a door-to-door insurance salesman. "What's the play, huh? You two gonna start beating me until I tell you something?"

Sheen grabbed Stone's face, turned it, forcing him to look at the spot across the room, where Etta had been strangled. "How'd you do it, Stone? Did you sneak up behind her or did you lunge at her and put your palms right on her throat," Sheen demanded!

Stone tried to turn his head away, but Sheen jerked it back, causing Stone a good deal of pain. He grunted but Sheen didn't care, he continued on with his allegations. "Did you stay around long enough for her stench to fill the room or did you run your candyass out of here the moment her body went limp?"

That last comment stuck in Stone's craw and he struck wildly at the detective's arms and broke Sheen's grasp from his head. "The nigger is dead and what difference does it make?" Stone's blood was up and it filled his cheeks as he continued, "She wasn't part of the plan!"

"And then you had me followed," Sheen added! "You were gonna try to put me away for the same crimes that Governor Eldridge committed?"

Stone barked back at him, "You're not my guy! He's a once in a generation mind, he could go all the way to Washington, maybe even the White House. I was gonna take the trip with him. You, I don't know. You're just a guy who couldn't play by the rules so he quit the cops."

The front door opened and shut and all three men in the kitchen heard it. Mickey looked over his shoulder, mostly using his peripheral vision. Stone saw him recognize that someone had entered the house and the Governor's chief of staff felt a sudden surge of confidence and sneered at Sheen.

"I gave her the opportunity to walk away! You think I wanted to see something like that happen?" Stone demanded. "It was a shame it had to come to that, but she refused to leave Eldridge's side and so I had to take extreme measures."

"And so you killed her," Sheen insisted.

"Yes! I did what had to be done," Stone declared.

Sheen smiled. "You fellas get that?" Sheen asked.

Stone's face grew curious, unsure who Sheen thought he was speaking to. Stone knew who had just entered the house. He had arranged for them to be waiting up the street, had given them the signal that they were to enter once he peeked through the kitchen blinds and knew they would be prepared to deal with Sheen and his friend in a manner similar to the way he'd handled Etta Childs.

So the surprise on Stone's face was to be expected when his two goons were escorted into the room, hands cuffed behind them and each with a gun at their back. Stone didn't recognize the two men who guarded his duo, but Sheen knew them as his former partner Detective Rupert Tierney and his old war buddy and current federal agent Richard Levesque.

"Yeah," the agent said. "We heard it."

Stone knew. He wasn't a stupid man, only cocky and a touch foolish. He had just confessed to murder and that admission was overheard by representatives of local and federal law enforcement. He shot a sideways glance at Sheen and grunted the words, "You son of a bitch."

Sheen had a sly smile on his face. The satisfaction of knowing the case was down, and that he'd caught the man who killed Etta Childs, brought its fair share of happiness. But he also enjoyed the fact that he could stick it to Stone, who he had, ultimately, come to the conclusion that he thoroughly disliked.

"Even a two-bit, back alley scrubber like me knows," Sheen smirked as he said, "As far as evidential proof is concerned, that's pretty good... you murdering shitbird."

Sheen grabbed Stone's arm and led him towards Tierney and Levesque.

Stone interjected, "Doesn't matter if it's me or if it's somebody else, gumshoe... You keep carrying on with that colored broad like that, it'll come out. Someone will do you for it. Just a matter of time."

Sheen looked over at Levesque. And though the agent may have been a little surprised to learn this fact he merely shrugged it off and said, "I didn't hear anything about that." Then Sheen turned his attention to Tierney. His old police partner was shocked, no idea what to say or do, and he certainly couldn't approve of this behavior.

Sheen, though concerned, reasoned with his old friend, mentioning, "Partners look out for each other."

Tierney let the moment of surprise have its due presence, then held his free hand up, all five fingers outstretched and shook his head. As if to say he wanted no part of that. All he verbally gave Sheen was, "You watch your ass."

Mickey grabbed Stone's arms and held his wrists together, following Tierney and Levesque out of the house. Sheen watched as the three closest friends he'd had in his life, then and now, took Etta's killer and his two flunkies out of the house.

He took one last look at the kitchen floor, thinking that he couldn't wait to tell Serena that the man who killed her sister, and was most likely behind the murder of her brother, was going to have to answer for his crimes. Just as Sheen would have to give some answers to a couple people.

He turned off the kitchen light and walked through the house, closing the front door behind him, knowing his next steps were to fill Josh Riley in on the details and have a conversation with Governor Eldridge.

CHAPTER 21

THE END OF IT

"**I** knew of Wendell, but obviously I'd never met him. Or Henrietta's sister. She spoke about them often... and with great affection."

Governor Eldridge sat at his desk, recalling anything he could about Wendell Childress. Across from his desk, sitting with a note-pad open in front of him, was Detective Sheen.

"He was a good fellow," Sheen offered in regards to Wendell. "And their sister is a very lovely woman."

The Governor merely nodded and Sheen read nothing on his face that indicated he had any knowledge of Sheen's relationship with Serena. Ultimately Sheen felt that Eldridge wouldn't care one way or another if he did know, but the detective wanted to have a sense of who had what information about him. At this point he was satisfied believing that Stone, Fisk and perhaps Stone's gunmen might be the only ones who had that knowledge.

"I want you to tell me everything you know," Eldridge insisted.

"Well, sir," Sheen prepared for it, "What I know is that Jensen Stone murdered Etta Childs. From what I can piece together, he decided to end your relationship for you. Had he, at some point, tried to talk you out of seeing Ms. Childs?"

"Several times. And it wouldn't take. I guess the last refusal was more than he could handle. What about the brother?"

"Wendell... He was, I believe, murdered under Stone's orders. A local police lieutenant, name of Granville, is believed by the department to have killed Mr. Childress. The reasons why are not entirely clear, but it's believed that... once I told him about your affair with his sister, he may have spoken out about it. Timing of the murder is too coincidental. And we now know that Granville had dealings with Jensen Stone. The authorities are trying to get a proper confession out of him, but he did admit to me, one of my associates, a federal agent and a Miami homicide detective that he killed Etta. We're just waiting to see if he comes clean on the rest."

Eldridge closed his eyes, slowly shook his head and said, "Jensen Stone. Jesus, I never would have thought he'd do something like this."

"There's another matter. Jonah Fisk," Sheen said.

Eldridge looked up at him and wanted to ask, but he didn't bother to make the words come out. But the sadness in his face asked the question all the same.

Sheen nodded and reported, "When he was killed, he had come to see me. And this Granville fellow and another man were sent to kill the both of us. I was lucky, but Jonah took the brunt of the shots that were fired into my office window. Sir, I believe very strongly that Jensen Stone was behind that kill order as well."

The Governor shook his head and mumbled, "I've spent much of my life, day after day for the past few years with a man like that."

Sheen continued, "Governor, I wanted to tell you all of this face to face. I wanted to give you the opportunity to decide how you would prefer to handle it."

"Meaning publicly," the Governor confirmed.

"I'm giving you the chance to come clean before I go to the papers. I don't care if you tell the story or if I tell the story, but it's got to come out."

Eldridge frowned, worry took over his expression and he stared off into cerebral solitude. Sheen tried his best to reassure Eldridge by saying, "Sir, you had no knowledge that Stone was doing these things. You stand to have no legal trouble."

"And perception?" Eldridge honestly asked. And Sheen gave an honest answer in the form of a shrug. He couldn't guarantee that the court of public opinion would be on his side in the matter.

"My chances of re-election, once they find out I was with a black woman... I don't agree with Jensen's actions... but he knew what he was doing."

Sheen felt, at that moment, that Eldridge was a very cold man. Could protection of his political career justify the murder of someone he'd loved? Eldridge caught Sheen's disapproving stare and explained, "I don't mean it that way. It's reprehensible what Stone did. But maybe that was his job, being reprehensible. I don't know... But I know that, no matter why she was killed, I get no peace from the truth. And I can't mourn Henrietta again. It was too painful the first time. I'm just not that strong."

Sheen understood. He didn't question Nate's love for Etta. It was simply that their love was victimized by power and could not conquer the impossible situation they found themselves in.

"I'll release a statement today," Eldridge said. "That should be out to the associated press for the late editions. It will be brief, disclosing my relationship with Etta. The rest I leave up to you."

Sheen nodded and mentioned, "I'm going to Josh Riley, your former employee."

The Governor's eyes lit up a little upon hearing the name. He'd always liked Riley and said, "Oh, really?"

"Yes. I think he'll write something fair. Honest, but fair about Stone and whatever degree to which he feels your relationship with Ms. Childs need be included."

Eldridge smiled, genuinely appreciative of the gesture and said, "Thank you, Detective."

Sheen nodded, stood and said, "I had better get along."

Eldridge stood, walked around to the front of his desk and shook Sheen's hand. He left Ben with the open invitation to call on him should he ever have any problem that the Governor could help with.

By the time Sheen had gotten back to Miami, the story of Florida Governor Nathaniel Eldridge and Negro star Etta Childs had been sent over the AP wire and was all over the state, as well as many of the bigger cities throughout the country.

When Sheen pulled his Coupe into the driveway of his house, he noticed another car sitting there. He recognized the familiar vehicle and entered his home feeling no need to be cautious.

"Hey there. How did everything go?" asked Mickey, comfortably sitting on Sheen's sofa.

"As good as can be expected," Sheen responded as he shut and locked the door behind him. "The Governor was upset by the news, but he stood up like a man does and issued a statement yesterday afternoon."

"Yeah, I know," Mickey replied. "It's been all over the news."

"I imagine. Well, we're about to knock it off the front page. Give me a minute will you?"

Mickey nodded and Sheen walked into the kitchen. He picked up the phone and dialed a number. Josh Riley answered and Sheen took the next twenty minutes to fill in the once and future reporter. He gave Riley all the salient details on Eldridge's relationship with Etta, Stone's involvement with Lt. Granville in Miami and the murders of Wendell Childress, Jonah Fisk and Etta Childs.

After he'd hung up with Riley, Sheen called Tierney and discussed the Granville matter. Tierney said that Granville was likely to be dishonored as a policeman and the public statement about it would be issued in the coming weeks.

Sheen had finished his calls and loosened his tie. He walked towards the living room and asked, "Were you able to do what I asked?"

"Yeah. She's in there sleeping," Mickey answered as he gestured down the hall.

"And Pearl?"

"She's got friends in her neighborhood looking after her. She's doing as best as can be expected under the circumstances."

Sheen nodded and said, "Thanks, Mick."

"Sure thing, pal," Mickey responded.

Sheen walked down the hall and turned into his bedroom. He saw a vision of loveliness, Serena lying with her feet curled up against her legs on his bed. On the floor, next to the bed, a few feet away was her protector... a brown and white bull terrier named Doyle.

Sheen smiled to see the familiarity of the moment. He walked closer and gently touched her feet. They felt cold in his warm hands so he reached for a blanket that was folded at the foot of the bed and covered her exposed legs, up to the shins.

He leaned in towards her sleeping body, saw a curl of black hair that was resting on her eye socket, and brushed it back away from her face. He kissed her cheek and, as he inhaled his next breath, caught a hint of her perfume and the smell that he usually detected on her neck.

Sheen grinned, happy to again be in her presence, but did not want to disturb her slumber. He quietly patted Doyle on the head and walked out of the room. Doyle did not follow his master, but rather stayed lying by the woman they had both welcomed into their home.

CHAPTER 22

EVER AFTER... ?

Doyle awoke when he heard a rustling of fabric. He opened his eyes to see the sheets on the bed next to him shift twice before two shapely, dark brown legs came into view. The two feet touched the ground before him and walked in the opposite direction, after which the rest of Serena was visible. Doyle stood up, stretched his canine body and followed her down the hall.

Once in the kitchen, Serena looked down and saw her companion standing by her feet. She bent down and scratched the top of his head, followed by a welcome scratch behind his left ear. His short tail wagged in appreciation.

"How about some breakfast?" Serena asked.

Doyle didn't understand her words, but the tone with which she said them sounded positive and he thought there might be food as a result of it. He sat in his place a few feet away from the stove, ever looking up to see the progress of his meal being prepared.

"Good morning," was spoken by Sheen and followed by a yawn. He had just entered the room, not long after having awoken. He moved towards Serena and placed his hand on her hip and took her mouth with a long, loving kiss. "How did you sleep?"

Serena smiled and responded, "Very well."

Sheen smiled and headed for the front door. The newspaper boy must have had a good arm today, as the morning edition was rested on the stoop, a mere foot and a half from the front door.

He picked up the newspaper and went back inside the house, leaving the main door open, but the screen door closed. He plopped the paper on his dining table and reached into the refrigerator for a bottle of orange juice. He poured a half of a glass and set it on the table. He began to read through the day's news.

It was September 27th and it had been several weeks since Governor Eldridge had publicly admitted to his relationship with Etta. Several weeks since Josh Riley's first article was published in the Miami News about the whole complex affair surrounding her murder, as well as the eventual murders of her brother and of Jonah Fisk. Riley also had a couple of follow up articles on the matter. Including one write-up on Stone's confession of ordering the deaths of Wendell and Fisk. Sheen later learned, from Riley, that the outright confessions were bartered by Stone in exchange for life imprisonment, instead of execution. Sheen was fine with that because he felt the long, slow torture of incarceration was worse than death and he thought Stone deserved it. The paper that Sheen currently read, The Miami Herald, didn't have as much on the Etta Childs case, as Josh Riley had the most information on the ordeal and he worked for the town's evening paper.

But Sheen was reading an article about a disgraced police officer, former lieutenant Mortimer Granville. After his death a great deal of dirt had been dug up on him and shown to the city of Miami, including his involvement in several murders and the attempted murder of a local private investigator. All this occurred just as Rupert had said it would the last time he and Sheen had spoken.

After he'd caught up with the so-called serious news, he turned to the sports page and saw that the Yankees had clinched the American

League pennant the day before when they beat the Philadelphia Athletics 5-2. There were still two games left in the season, but the World Series matchup was already decided, with the Dodgers having clinched the National League championship a couple days earlier.

"Dodgers are going to the World Series to play the Yankees again," Sheen commented. "Brooklyn baseball, boy... they must be sadists."

He grinned and looked up to find Serena placing a bowl in front of an expectant Doyle. Its contents: a ham and Swiss sandwich with shortbread cookies covered in milk. The dog gobbled it up as Serena watched on, slightly shaking her head. She looked over at Sheen, a touch of disapproval in her eyes and remarked, "That can't be good for him."

Sheen shrugged it off. Serena walked past him en route to the living room, placing a loving hand on his shoulder as she walked by. She stood at the front door and looked out through the screen.

Sheen returned his attention to his sports page and saw an advertisement for wrestling airing live from Miami. Clete "The Crusher" vs. "Russian Red" Raliokov! Sheen recognized "The Crusher" as Clete Tompkins, who had months earlier been a legitimate boxer, heart-broken by Etta Childs. Sheen remembered he had questioned the kid's killer instinct and reckoned Clete must have realized he wasn't cut out for boxing after all, and converted to a career in staged fighting.

Thinking about Clete made Sheen think about Etta, and how talented she was and how lovely a woman she seemed to be, and that it was an awful tragedy for her to be gone from this earth. He thought about Nathaniel Eldridge and how, in just over a month from now, he would likely lose his re-election campaign in a landslide. That was assuming Eldridge didn't withdraw his candidacy in the meantime. Sheen wasn't sure what kind of governor Delmar Wiggins of

Alachua County would make, but Sheen knew that his vote was going to Nathaniel Eldridge.

He also thought about Jonah Fisk and what a decent man he was, clinging to principals and good old-fashioned manners amidst the quagmire of political sleaze and scandal.

And when he thought of decency in man, he thought on Wendell Childress. The man who had first brought the case of Etta Childs to his doorstep. He hadn't known Childress all that well, but what little time he had spent with the man was something that Sheen cherished. He liked Wendell's philosophy of life and appreciated the good and simple things they had in common. And Sheen's fondest memory of Wendell would always be the time they spent talking at a backyard barbecue, where he had been welcomed to the man's home, which was a basic kindness Sheen felt no one should ever take for granted.

As Sheen thought of the greatest thing that had happened to him as a result of Wendell stepping into his office, he looked up at Serena, her soft gaze focused on the world outside his door.

"My, it is a beautiful day, isn't it?" she commented. After one final look, she stepped away from the door and took a seat on the sofa. Sheen stared at her, deeply in love, knowing she wasn't looking at him and thinking that whether she looked at him or not, he could spend the rest of his life watching her.

He stood from his chair, walked to the kitchen and retrieved two glasses from the cupboard. He had a bottle of lemonade in the fridge that had just been freshly squeezed the previous afternoon. He filled both glasses with ice and poured the liquid into each of them. Then he walked towards the front door.

He opened the screen door with the side of his body and stood in front of it to keep it from closing. With a glass in each hand he said to Serena, "Come on."

She had a puzzled expression on her face, not sure where he was asking her to go. But a gesture of his head indicating towards the front porch spelled it out and she stood up. She walked to the front door, raising her eyebrows at him as she passed.

"Have a seat," he suggested. She obliged and sat in one of the two chairs that were separated by a small table. Sheen approached, letting the door close from its own weight, and handed Serena one of the glasses. He sat next to her.

Serena took a sip of her lemonade and looked at the street out front, the houses across the way and the surrounding sky. Sheen reached across to Serena, intertwined his fingers with hers and pulled her arm closer. Serena gave Sheen a look that clearly said she wasn't so sure about this.

Sheen shrugged and told her, "Hell with 'em. We'll outlive 'em."

Serena smiled, familiar with that motto. Sheen took a sip of his lemonade and they enjoyed the first of many cool, fresh autumn breezes.

ABOUT THE AUTHOR

Lifelong Miami resident David Sayre turns his attention from independent films to writing novels with his first published novel, *Some Are Shadows*. Sayre previously wrote and directed several short films and wrote articles on film and television for the now defunct Internet magazine *Pictures and Frames*. Sayre remains loyal to his Miami Heat and Los Angeles Dodgers and plays poker in his spare time. Readers can follow him on Twitter @writtenbysayre and on his website at davidsayre.net.